FALLEN TREES

FALLEN TREES

A BOOK OF SHORT STORIES

Loren L. Qualls
Author of *Dark Language*

iUniverse, Inc.
New York   Bloomington

FALLEN TREES
A BOOK OF SHORT STORIES

Copyright © 2008 by Loren L. Qualls

This is a work of fiction. All of the characters, names, incidents, organizations,
and dialogue in these short stories are either the products of the author's
imagination or are used fictitiously.

iUniverse books may be ordered through booksellers or by contacting:

iUniverse
1663 Liberty Drive
Bloomington, IN 47403
www.iuniverse.com
1-800-Authors (1-800-288-4677)

Because of the dynamic nature of the Internet, any Web addresses or links
contained in this book may have changed since publication and may no longer be
valid. The views expressed in this work are solely those of the author and do not
necessarily reflect the views of the publisher, and the publisher hereby disclaims
any responsibility for them.

ISBN: 978-0-595-52662-8 (pbk)
ISBN: 978-0-595-62716-5 (ebk)

Printed in the United States of America

The analogous evolution of post-rebellion fiction:

…Envisage of parents moaning and cooing while footing around some plantation, demeaning them-selves in a *step-in-fetch-it* slave rendering. The two visions turn to a small *black-faced* boy and push him out and off the plantation. He kicks as he screams to stay and as he cries the *blackface* begins to run and soon it all washes away, leaving him featureless. The boy walks blindly for a time; then bumping into the world or as Heidegger might say, "Experiencing *Dasien*" which means *being-in-the-world,* a nose pops forward then an eye and so on. The boy is learning, absorbing all that life offers until his face completely forms, nevertheless, when he stands in front of the mirror he does not recognize himself.

—*The vision*

Contents

MORROW FALLING

The first time I realized my father was a great man was the morning after my mother had gone back to Ohio for a funeral. The night before I was afraid to sleep alone and he let me sleep with him, but the proof of greatness didn't come until morning.

The sun moved over the room like tiny fingers crawling over someone's back; small hands looking for a place to nestle and grab hold. My parents had an enormous bed that stretched out forever. I could start at one end and begin to roll and I would always have to stop and take a break before reaching the other side. I was at the far end of the bed and my father's back seemed distant and indifferent. He'd worked late the night before and I had fallen asleep waiting for him in the den. My older brother had waited with me but I guess he must have tired and went to bed. I just know I woke-up in my parent's room feeling annoyed by the sun and alone. Mommy was gone and my father seemed so far away. How could I even be sure that that was my father? I couldn't see his face. I could only see this hump under the covers. So I looked beneath the sheet finding two hairy legs, but they may not be his. My

Dad has a birthmark on the back of his left thigh and both my brother and I share the same marking. I couldn't find the area of shaded skin, it was too dark under the covers and I didn't want to wake him by moving too much. Daddy wouldn't care if I moved, but the stranger might. At first I sat motionless, waiting for this clump of sheet and blanket to turn into something recognizable, other than the floral patterns that aided in its obscurity. He's really gone…who's going to take me to McDonald's on Saturday's and read story's to me after school until Mommy comes home? If I try to sneak out he might wake up and be angry…and you can never tell how strangers will act. If I scream my brother might hear and come and get me before the stranger can. I wonder if my brother already knows Daddy's gone. He wouldn't care because he thinks I'm Dad's favorite. He may even be thrilled. My nose began to burn and it was like domino's, the corners of my mouth bent down, my brow pinched and my vision blurred as the tears welled up in my eyes. I swallowed hard to keep from crying out.

I moved closer, reaching out, touching his back and he didn't move. He breathed heavily just as my hand touched his shoulder and it startled me causing me to pull away. A draft fanned the room and the intensity of the sun grew but the room felt cold and sterile. The tears had already dried making my face feel hard and chapped. The stranger was still there and I knew now crying wouldn't help.

The room was beginning to glow with the sun's luminance. It carried the sun's light without its warmth. Shivering, I sat up and stared at the hump as it stretched and shrank mocking my father's presence. I watched this stranger a bit longer and then I scrunched under the covers to escape the morning chill. And that's when the stranger stretched his hand back and pulled me close. My face rested on the wide of his back shading me from the enveloping light. This was my father, and he was great. The sun in all its magnitude could not burn the chill from the room, but I found warmth in my father's shadow.

FALLEN TREES

Post-rebellion fiction takes a critical examination of African-Americans at the decline of the African-American civil rights era and asks, "Now that we know the antagonists mind and live in the adversaries' house, eat our enemies' food, who are we?"

The rain, like fragile jewels shattered against the windowpanes, car hoods, and crowded streets of the district. I watched in awe of nature's beauty and fierceness. The thunder rolls by my office window; a breeze held the blind in an upward curve on its left side then snatches it back down with a metallic slap. The heavy and dank smell of wet cement tickles the inside of my nose. An electric vein flashes across the expanse of space, rumbling without consideration of the pedestrians running, clutching their umbrella's tightly, feeling the wetness of the ground seeping into their shoes, corrupting their socks, stockings and exposed feet.

I look down at my own feet, damp and cold. I could see a run in my stocking that starts at my baby-toe and moves up my thigh disappearing underneath my skirt. I scan the room focusing on the heels I had kicked off as I entered my office. I trace my steps along the carpet, holding a level of contempt and hatred for the carpet-tack aimed up in insolent rebellion. That mischievous tack had maimed, destroyed a perfectly good pair of stockings. I stood never taking my eyes off my intended; moving quietly, passing the front of my desk I took the stapler. I kneel in a slow bend and began to beat the tack into the floor. Each stroke landed with a hollow thump that lingered in the air above me. I was just about to clobber the tack-head for the tenth time when my door swung open.

"Miss Allyn, you all right? Oh excuse me, I'm sorry I didn't mean to...."

Looking up I said, "Russell? What is it Russell?"

"The Director wants you...I should have knocked, right? That's a shaarrp suit Miss Allyn, but you gotta' ah nasty run, don't you hate that?" Russell kept his eyes on the ensemble, "I wouldn't have barged in but I heard noises."

"Hm, yeah thanks. Call maintenance and have them come fix that?" I said getting off my knees and placing the stapler back on the desk. Russell nodded and stood to the side as I leaned against the wall to slip into my shoes. I could feel Russell watching me walk and I knew it was not just the suit or some hidden interest in me. I'm sure he is not ready or even willing to jeopardize his celebrity in the gay community, not for me. It's something else. I looked back at the pudgy well-dressed man before knocking on the director's door. Russell's cheeks trembled as he turned his gaze, acting as if he'd been fingering through the folders wrapped in his arm.

I tapped lightly on the door in front of me and waited. I stared at the marquis, letting my eyes follow the engraved lines that form, Marvin Gahl, Director, Federal Census Delegation of Inquiry.

"Come in. It's open." A voiced called.

I opened the door without apprehension. The director sat behind his cheery oak desk that seemed to extend from one end of the room to the other. The pinch-faced economist, holding strong to his 50's straightened his tie and ran his hand over his graying hair.

"Nina I'm glad to see you. You've been well? The work you've been doing here has been excellent."

"Thank you, sir."

"How long before you can get caught up?" He put his hands behind his head.

"I'm not sure sir. A few weeks maybe."

"Do you think one of the others can handle that?"

"I suppose they could but—"

"I need to send you to Flora, South Carolina."

"Where?"

"Flora, South Carolina."

"Why?"

"Well, your experience could be an asset in this case." He opened up a file on his desk and then turned and punched a few keys on his computer.

"What kind of case is it?"

"Well, it's complex but the numbers in this city seem to be dropping. The population is decreasing and it doesn't seem environmental or disease related, there are other agencies looking into it but they haven't had any conclusive results, as to why people are, well, basically disappearing."

"Maybe it's an extraterrestrial."

"C'mon Nina, let's be serious."

"Marvin, why am *I* going?"

"Nina you would think the world has changed but it hasn't in some places—"

"Marvin, what's your point?"

"Well out of all the candidates to send you were the most recognized."

"What? Please, there are plenty of agents that have been here longer and have been recognized far more times, and as a matter of fact my only real distinction is that I'm a woman and the only African-American woman working for the—"

Marvin cut his eye back at me keeping his head facing his computer.

"This is some—this isn't right—this is crap—you want to send me to Buttfunky, South Carolina because I'm black?"

"Listen Nina it's not just that, you're qualified, but the climate in Flora calls for specific provisions and we thought this would help." Marvin's gaze danced around my face avoiding my eyes.

"WE?"

"The powers that be; besides it's not that different from DC, except the economics. The dominant or rather the power structure is mainly African-American."

"Oh, you mean somewhere we are finally running the show? Well, that is somethin'. You can't find anyone else?" I imagine Russell's evasive eyes and figure he must have known. He could have warned me. I would have gone home sick.

"Nope, not in our department; you are it." After saying this Marvin finally let his eyes meet mine and he smiled. I wanted to slap him.

Flora, South Carolina appeared no different than any other city. The view from the plane showed the familiar patterns of streets and buildings, outlined by strategically placed lights. The evening sky showed of orange and purple that fell on the horizon, as the shadowed earth heaved up to meet the heavens. I noticed but the desire to be off the plane crowded this sentiment to the back my mind. I kept thinking where do I begin? I wondered about the people I would meet; what they are thinking right now in anticipation of my arrival, whether they were concerned or indifferent?

I walked the exit ramp to the gate. I could see a thin white youth standing by a row of pay phones. He wasn't much to look at but his shoes caught my attention. I hadn't seen a pair of red converse high-tops in years at least not since my *tomboy* days at George Washington High. I was "Gochi", short for *go child*. A nickname my father started calling me at my track meets. He would stand with his fists clinched, screaming *go chi*, screaming to me, the fastest freshmen at George Washington and in the city and the world! Well, at least I thought I was the fastest thing movin' at the time.

I kept my hair pulled back in a ponytail and for everyday wear, sweatpants, a T-shirt and red all-star converse. Running was all that mattered and dressing up to be Mommy and Daddy's little girl meant nothing to me. My parents would beg and plead, offering me monetary rewards if I would just once look like a lady. My mother would just shake her head and say I was wasting all the beauty god had given me. Now, my father would agree but I knew he was quietly relieved that boys had not discovered the beauty my mother found so evident. But the day came when his relief would end. It came by way of Kenny Knight or K.K. that's what everyone called him. He was a great runner and a junior. Tall, lanky, chocolate brown, ooh, he was fine—a beautiful black man. Well, a boy then but still fine. I'm not sure if he was fine because he was one of the best athletes at George

Washington or because he was older. Everyone thought Kenny was the stuff; maybe that was it. The first time Kenny had ever said anything to me was right at the end of a track meet and we were leaving the field. I was putting my running shoes in my bag along with a towel and a water bottle. He was sitting on the lower bleacher changing his shoes. He stared at me for a long time. I could feel him looking, it annoyed me at first then it became irritating and then I was just pissed. So, I asked, "Do you have a problem?" He kept watching me for a moment and said, "You know if you do somethin' with your hair, put on some different clothes you'd be kinda' cute." I snubbed him without acknowledging his words; smirking picking up my duffel bag pretending his opinion meant nothing. Later, I found myself standing in front of the bathroom mirror roaming my face. I traced the shape of my eyes and the contour of my cheeks and jaw, along with my mouth and lips with the hopes of discovering the beauty my mother urged that god had given me. After awhile I thought, what did Kenny know that bratha' is wearin' a curl.

The skinny boy shifts his feet and the red blurred briefly drawing my attention back into the present. I notice he is leaning in one of the booths but he isn't using the phone. As I pass, he picks up the handset and begins to speak without dialing any numbers. I think the kid is weird.

A taxi takes me to the hotel the Bureau had reserved. The taxi slows in front of the Regency Vista. I step from the taxi and stand while the driver retrieves my bags from the trunk. The humidity crawls up my neck, itches the skin of my spine with tiny beads of perspiration. I need to get out of these stockings, this bra. If it's this hot now, during the day the heat must be relentless. I turn to the taxi driver.

"Do you know the weather for tomorrow?"

"Ah, the radio say hot, hot, hot, and it might rain in thah' evenun'." He said looking up and around.

A bellhop picked up my bags and placed them on a cart.

"This all mam?"

"Yes. Is it always this hot?" I ask. The bellhop smiled as he pulled the cart inside the hotel lobby, "Yep, hot like this all the way tuh Christmas."

"This is June."

"I know, welcome tuh' Flora."

I walked through the automatic doors stopping at the front desk to check-in. The clerk, an average sized man with brown skin smiled brightly.

"How may we help you this evenun'?"

"I'd like to get the key to my room. There should be a reservation for Allyn."

He pecked a few keys on the computer keyboard, tightened his lips and squints

his eyes as he stared at the computer screen. "Ah, here you go, right here, room 334, let me code yah key-card." He motioned to the bellhop to take my bags up.

"Mrs. Allyn you have a message too."

"It's Miss and thanks."

"I'm Todd Works the manager. If you need anythun', anyyythuun at all just call the front desk." He was grinning so hard I could see his gums.

"Thanks Todd, I'll do that."

I followed the bellhop to the elevator and as we rode up to the third floor I read the message:

Welcome to Flora.
10:00 AM briefing @ The Cordell Building.
Office liaison: Harper Sims
Mr. Sims will facilitate your transportation,
the Bureau District Office.

"3rd floor Miss Allyn." The bellhop said.

I fold the note and exit the elevator. I can feel fatigue pushing at the back of my eyes as I enter my hotel room. The humidity is weighing me down. The blast of air conditioning surrounds and lifts me and I feel as if I am floating.

"Well, if you want anything else just ring-up room service. Pleasant night."

The bellhop stood there patiently. "Could you bill it to the room?" I said.

"Yes, thank you," he said with a nod and smile. He knew charging the room would guarantee his full gratuity.

The door shut and I went straight for the shower, coming out of my clothes with each step. I stand in front of the mirror already in my bra and panties. I stop and stare, running my hands over my hair. The shortness of my hair in some ways made me look less professional, I thought. Maybe it is the untamed quality of the curls and with the humidity this would be the only hairstyle that I could possibly wear or that would wear me. I guess this trip would be all natural; wash and wear. I pull one of the curls straight, down to the tip of my nose and let it go. I watch it spring back into a coiled configuration affirming the hopelessness of the *hair question*. No matter, in and out of the shower and to bed.

The phone rang at 7:30 AM; it scares the crap out me. I'd forgotten that I arranged a wake-up call. I sit up and grab for the remote clicking on the television.

"Good morning South Carolina. It's half past the hour and it looks like it's going to be another hot one today. Temperatures reaching the upper 90's and the low for tonight will be a humid 73 degrees. Stay cool and have pleasant day."

"Thanks Bob. Just in, another body has been found in the Flora marsh. This is the 7th in what appears to be an assortment of arbitrary killings in the Flora County area. A group of college students camping in the marsh discovered the body around 4:00 AM. The body has not yet been identified but we do know that the victim was a female approximately 45 to 50 years of age."

I listened causally to the news and then clicked to another channel and then another. It's all news, local news, the nation's news, and world news. It's 7:40 AM and I was already feeling like I was behind. I feel like it is too late; too late to sign up and live. The decision regarding who gets to play in life has already been made. Just like being sent here and the outcome of the case is already determined. I don't know this for sure but it's just a feeling, a feeling that everything around me is schemed in someway. Maybe knowing how and why I'm in Flora has tainted my perspective.

I take a shower and quickly wash my hair and body, towel off, brush my teeth and let my hair air-dry, while I putting on my face. It is going to be too hot for a suit. The khaki Capri's, a white cotton-knit tank and canvass shoes, will do. Not much later I'm in the lobby.

"Todd's gone?" I said, noticing the change in the desk clerk.

The woman looks up from writing and pauses from chewing her gum like cow cud and then she begins again.

"Whachu need?" She smacks.

"I was asking about Todd the desk clerk. He was here last night."

"Yeah, he work at night. He be in later." She pops a bubble and returns to her writing.

"We'll I want to know if I had any messages?" The clerk stiffens letting her face fall into an expressionless glob.

"Do I?" I pressed.

"Do yah' what?"

"Do I have any messages," letting my voice go up at the end.

"Oh, let me check." She turned swinging her hair which was a blonde and brown mingle that I'm sure she bought from an Asian owned store, specializing in the *black experience*: such as velvet paintings of panthers, elephant statues, the Black-Jesus-Last- Supper, incense named Black Liquorish or Egyptian love. She pushed the few strands that fell back in her face away from her forehead with her acrylic nails. As I watched her I noticed she held her hands as if they were hurting. I cleared my throat.

"Waydah minute. I just got my nails did and I don't wanna chip um'." The desk clerk squeaks.

"Excuse me. Um Mam? I'm—" A man spoke from the other end of the counter, "I'm supposed to pick-up a Nina Allyn, could you ring her room?"

"Waydah menut, jus' wait, I'm doin' sun'in' rot now!" The desk clerk rattled.

I heard my name and looked up from the clerk, "I'm Nina Allyn."

"Oh it's a pleasure. I'm Harper Sims Miss…" He extended his hand. "Miss Allyn I hope you slept well and your accommodations, expectable?"

"Everything's fine." I said watching the motion of his angular jaw as he spoke. His brown skin, though natural you could see that the sun had been working on improving Mr. Sims' looks. His hair was a mess of curls, sort of like mine with the exception that his seemed to be working on an artistic level, coordinating with his bare lip and goatee. Obviously I thought he was all right. Mr. Harper was a long way from Kenny and the others that followed. Kenny became my first boyfriend after he got rid of his gerry-curl. We began dating at the end of my freshmen year. He graduated and went onto college and of course Kenny realized my high school world lacked the sophistication of college life. Like drinking and fucking.

"You work for the Bureau?" I asked.

"Yeah, why?" Harper smiled and I could see the dimple in his left cheek.

"You don't look like the Bureau. I mean your wearing flip-flops and ear-rings." "Maybe this is my cover, eh?"

"Oh really?"

"Yeah, this sorta' hip-hop-artist type bratha', wild hair and sandals, oh don't forget the sideburns," he chuckled. "No, really I'm a short fat white guy with a receding hair line."

"Well, if that's the case why this cover?"

"Don't you know, you gotta' be down tah' get down in Flora." Harper laughed aloud as he passed through the revolving doors of the hotel. I followed, passing through the sucking air that wisped cool and unencumbered turning to smoldering slaps that burned with each step into the morning sun. I wondered if he knew they sent me to Flora because I was black?

"I guess you haven't eaten yet?" Harper said getting into the car without opening the door for me.

"No but I can wait for lunch. We should be getting to the meeting."

As we drove something moved up and through me and I began suffocate. I felt as if I were wrapped in a hundred blankets with cotton shoved in my nose and a light of immense intensity has been directed into the whole of the blanket where my face peeks out at the world. I am helpless. I am feverish. The heat is killing me.

"Harper, turn the air on!" I heard myself yelling in desperation. "It's hot as h---. It's hot!"

"Air? The air is on. Give it a minute to get cool."

I let the window down and a blast of invisible fire singed the side of my face. "It must be hundred degrees."

Harper pulled off to the side and put the car in park.

"This is the best parking I can get, downtown can be busy."

"Is this the Cordell?"

"No, it's about a block up."

"I'm gonna have a stroke in this heat."

"C'mon it's not that far."

"Okay but lets find some shade for a minute."

We walked for about five minutes, then ten minutes.

"Harper when are we going to get to a nice shade tree or somethin'?"

"Tree? They're no trees in Flora, hasn't been for years. Not since the *Inversion Act of 1968*."

We arrived at the Cordell building a few scorching minutes later and I am still wondering what Harper meant. It was so hot outside I didn't have the energy to ask him to explain the Inversion Act or more importantly why the hell he stopped at the street vendor to buy a paper in this heat. But once the air conditioning of the Cordell building hit me I honestly no longer cared.

"This is Nina Allyn from the bureau's office in Washington." Harper introduced me to a woman and three men seated around a long table in a room filled with books and old paintings.

"Hi, I'm Mildred Dryford and this is Henton Beeks and Chief Willard Kline." The woman stood and motioned with her hand for me to sit across from her. "Miss Allyn we would like to get right to the point. I represent the Mayors office and the Chief is here of course from the Police Department and Mr. Beeks is from the State Department." I could tell almost immediately that Mildred did not like what I was wearing. She grimaced, as she looked me from head to toe. "You and Mr. Harper should get along quite well. You appear to have a lot in common. You know working for the bureau; you both seem, casual, comfortable."

"If I may ask, why do you need so many branches of government for a census report?" I asked.

Mildred and the others looked at each other. Harper who had been reading the newspaper looked up as if stunned by the silence.

"How much have you been told about what's going on here?" Mr. Beeks leaned forward lacing his fingers.

"Only what the report revealed and what my office has instructed." I said.

The Chief spoke after clearing his throat, "Miss Allyn this is not just about the numbers of people it's about numbers of dollars."

Mildred pursed her lips together hard. It looked as if she were holding something back, something fighting to get out. I hadn't noticed until then how the darkness of her complexion hid the wrinkles about her mouth.

"Miss Allyn, Flora is an historical city and we don't want these events to become so public that it hurts the city. We feel there are factions that would seek to exploit and destroy what Flora has become and represents."

"Well, I can understand if you don't want people knowing that the city is losing a portion of its constituency that could cost, voter wise and tax wise…" I began.

"No, listen…" Mr. Beeks interjected, "Since the Inversion Act of 1968, Flora has made strides in the community of cities and these strides brought the city millions of dollars. This was not only impressive but considered extraordinary for a city run by *us*."

"The Inversion Act of 1968, could someone bring me up to speed here?" I leaned back in my chair letting my eyes circle the room empty faces—practiced expressions, much like the paintings on the walls. Everyone in the room was black. Every painting on the wall portrayed an historical Black American.

"You see, the Act shifted the balance of power in this city, setting a precedent for this country. The Act forced black ownership of white businesses that had been in someway established, built or maintained by any oppressive acts against Black Americans. This act made the businesses the immediate property of that oppressed group, making them automatic shareholders. This act, which we believe was an experiment that government officials thought would fail, helped Flora flourish, at a time when there was nothing in Flora worth anything. That's why they did it. They didn't want us to begin to riot like every other city in the Country. So this was the deal." Beeks looked at me as if he were sending some telepathic message. I wasn't getting it.

"If it's been so successful why hasn't anyone else in the country heard about Flora?" I said letting my eyes settle on Harper. The newspaper had fallen forward and his attention was now on us.

"That was part of the agreement. If the deal was to be accepted there could be no media attention, no publicity." Beeks seemed tired when he said this. It was almost as if he were worn out from making this same argument a thousand times before. "If there is any indication that the city is failing under its current leadership the contract becomes void and the government claims everything we have worked for." Beeks ended.

"Everything for nothing." Mildred adds.

"Things will just go back the way they were, maybe even worse." The Chief said.

"But, what does this have to do with my office?"

Harper sat up letting the paper fall to the table. His expression showed *epiphany*, "She doesn't know about the murders does she?"

"Miss Allyn, we need you to put together a report reflecting the moderate changes in the over all populace without the focus being the velocity of the decrease." Mildred watched my face for an opening of agreement.

"Murders?" I said without taking my eyes away from Mildred's pruned mouth. It began to look like an asshole.

"Yeah, there was another reported last night. Local news confirmed it this morning." Harper looked around the table waiting for one of the three to substantiate his remarks.

The Chief began to point and wave his finger. His mouth opened, moving up and down without producing a single sound. Then finally, Beeks said, "Mr. Sims there is no need to panic Miss Allyn."

"Oh I'm not panicked, just confused. Let me see if I understand. I was brought here to assess and write a report on the declining numbers of your cities population. But you want that report to reflect the stability of Flora's numbers, which I guess would be a fabrication because of the murders. But without a positive report Flora loses its creditability and *Big Brother* comes in and takes back everything that the Inversion Act provided. Is that about right?"

"Well, yes. We just need a little time to catch those responsible; just enough time for that. I've got people working on it and they're close." The Chief had found his voice.

"You don't have to fabricate anything. Write the report when an arrest is made." Beeks said looking at the Chief.

"We didn't ask you to come here Miss Allyn, but since you're here allow us a little time." Mildred said.

I am motionless, unsure how long because of the numbness of my body. I want to go home, right now. I want to do the stupid report and go home. I can't move. If I move I'll end up at the airport on the first flight back to DC.

"Well why don't you take a couple of days to decide." Mildred said.

"A few days to think about it, that's all, just few days." The Chief said.

I looked them over.

"Miss Allyn." Harper said already standing at the door.

I stood, finally moving with a lucidness of someone in a trance. Then the final question of the day tumbled from my lips hitting the table breaking into syllables that bounced off its grain surface, landing in the faces of Flora's decision makers, "What happened to the trees?"

"Let's go." Harper urged.

"The trees?"

"They went with lynching?" Mildred said folding her arms across her chest.

"What?"

"We'll call to let you know our progress." The Chief said.

We arrived in front of the Regency Vista.

"What is wrong with Mrs. Dryford?"

"She's a little stiff." Harper laughed.

"Stiff? She's dead. The living-dead, sent here to inflict her evil on us." I said with a smirk.

"Well, I guess you'll be trying take in a little of Flora since you have the time?" Harper tried to sound casual between laughs.

"Why not start right now?" I said.

"Yeah, why not, I know this place." He drove, smiling as if he knew a big secret. After a few minutes we pulled into a parking lot a block from the hotel. We stopped and he got out, motioning for me to follow. I noticed a small structure that reminded me of a parking-attendant-booth or the old Kodak film booths only with and extra room. We rounded the building and the window slid back and a young woman leaned out.

"Sup' 'arper? Whacanah getchall? Ah mean, welcome to Edna's Burger and ice-cream."

"I guess you come here a lot?"

"Yeah, this is my spot. What would you like?"

"Here I am thinking we're going to happy hour" I smiled, "Hmm they got any pistachio?"

"Let me get a scoop of lime sherbet in a sugar-cone and a scoop of pistachio in the same."

The young woman handed Harper our orders, each wrapped in an Edna's napkin. We walked back the car in silence, lost in the simplicity of the frozen substance and its complex effect on our tongues at least that's what I was thinking. Harper already had sherbet dripping done his chin. I unwrapped the napkin from my cone and before I could offer it, Harper was chuckling facetiously, "Look at your cone." He said. She had given me a plain ordinary cone. Not a sugar-cone, just a cone.

"Well she tried, I guess." Harper ended.

We got in the car still half smiling. It didn't seem as hot and I wasn't as bothered by being in Flora anymore.

"Harper what did Mildred mean by *lynching*?" I leaned back in the car seat.

"They cut down all the trees as a reminder of the things that happened and to avoid a future that embraces lynching. This isn't the only time that Flora has had trouble with a shrinking population. Lynching at one time was the number one cause of death of Black Americans in Flora."

"But all the trees?" I said

"All but one."

I heard laughter from behind the car. It was coming from the booth. I looked back and I could see a young man leaning into the service window at Edna's. I couldn't see his face but he was wearing red all-star converse. Harper started the car and pulled off. I watched the red all-stars shift and pose.

"Who's the kid in the shoes?"

"What kid?"

"One of the only white people I've seen in Flora. He was at the booth."

"I don't know, I didn't see him."

By this time we had left the lot and entered into traffic. Harper drove towards the city limits. I watched the cityscape fade into a flat surface, tangled by brown grass and leaning fence-posts, twisted by time and natures unyielding will. The landscape flowed without deviation, without distraction of foliage; barren mounds rolled up and passed my face with the speed of the car. An eternal perspective leading my eyes; I feel as if I am rushing to meet the horizon, empty and cloudless. I find myself in a place where there is nothing above me or beneath me. And here I am, with nothing to reach for and nothing to stand on. My faith pours out to an empty heaven and my soul bares witness to a field of stones.

The car slowed and Harper said, "Come on I want you to see this." The sun had begun to slip beneath the deserted range. I watched for a moment and Harper called me again.

"Hey, look at this. This is it."

He stood over a stump. As I came closer I could see that it's a tree mangled and bent. The knotted growth formed like a seven, which had fallen over on its open side. It came up from a nest of matted roots holding to the soil like grasping fingers and then it curved down, as if it had decided to stand and fall all at once.

"This is it. This is the last, last Poplar tree in Flora." Harper looked almost sad. "The day the Inversion Act was passed a man was brought out here and beaten and skinned alive. Then the mob hung him and burned his remains as he dangled from the tree. I heard the tree bent from the weight, giving it this shape; almost like it laid the man's body down to rest along with all the hate and prejudice. The murderers were never caught and the whole thing was just ignored and now forgotten."

"White people can be pretty vicious?"

"White people? The only *white people* known to have been here was the mayor and he was hangin' from the tree." Harper said this as if he stood by and watched the atrocity and had done nothing, now many years later the guilt is overwhelming. He tried to smile; then he turned back to the car. "It was Flora's declaration of independence. Most of the white people left after that. The few that stayed where poor and couldn't go."

"Why are you here? Just for the Bureau?"

"Nah, I grew up here, went to college up north, graduated, worked for the bureau in Cleveland for a while, then my father got sick so I came home to help my mother. When my father died I requested a transfer and that was a year ago." Harper started the car, clicked on the headlights and hit the gas. The tires spun in the gravel before lunging forward onto the paved road.

"Why didn't the Bureau just let you handle this?"

"They thought I might be too close to it and working together adds a conscience to the report and that makes all interested parties feel at ease." He must have been doing hundred down this dark road as he spoke.

"A conscience, for who, you or me or should I say a conscience for whom, you or I?" I asked watching the road, smiling.

"Not for us, for them." He looked at me with a quick glance, ignoring my humor, "You feel like a drink?"

Tepid fingers of sunlight reach through the window and tap against my face, caressing the half not lost in the pillow. The warm light drums against my closed eye, lighting the lid like a neon veil causing me to squint and turn away from the window. I can taste last night's cocktails on my tongue. I know it's no use trying to go back to sleep, so I peek at the clock on the end table and it reads 1:05 PM. I push myself up and scan the room. Harper is curled up on the short couch beneath the window. I watch him breath in and out. The rhythm is captivating, slow hypnotic, calming. It feels natural for him to be here, sleeping. I'm surprised at this ease. I look down at my body to see if I'm still wearing my clothes.

"Ay, you're awake. How ya' feelin'?" Harper stretches and shifts his body on the couch. I smile thinking I need to brush my teeth. "Man, I'm starvin' you wanna get something to eat?" Harper continues.

"Yeah, that sounds good but I gotta' get myself together first."

"What time is it? I need to go take a shower myself." Harper said standing.

"Well, what do you wanna do?" The phone rang cutting my words off, "Excuse me one sec, hello. Hey Russell—progress? A few days—a couple days. When did the Director say he wanted me back? Monday? Today is only Thursday. I'll call-in on Sunday." I grab some clothes from my suitcase and walk toward the bathroom.

"I take it that was Washington calling." Harper said reaching for his pager that had begun to go off. "This must be my office calling." He read the text message on the small screen: Sims: Progress report: Meeting 1500 Hours***." Harper looked up from his pager, "I've gotta' go in for a meeting."

"Is it the district office? Maybe I should go with you?"

"No it's the committee. They code their messages with three stars."

"Oh, okay well, I'll see you later then. Besides I need to get started on a draft of the report for my office." I was feeling left out.

"I'll come back after the meeting and let you know what's going on." Harper closed the door behind him.

888

An hour had gone by and the screen to my laptop remained blank. Well, almost blank the exception being the computer generated a caricature of Einstein. He stood patiently with his hands behind his back, occasionally rocking up on his toes and back, yawning and clearing his throat. I watched him stupidly and he blinked. In the same callous manner I beat the carpet tack into the floor I clicked the program off. Einstein's eyes bulged and he sneezed, flying backwards into computerized oblivion, finally disappearing. I can't write a report from nothing. I need stats from the city for at least the last five years. Harper is taking too long. I open the door and step out into the hall and two men rush by me pushing and pulling an ambulance gurney.

I couldn't make out the face of the person strapped to the gurney. I could only see the blood, everywhere. Then the police, hands and badges running and forcing me back into my room. I went to the window and I could see the paramedics loading the ambulance. The police stood around as if guarding the identity of the victim or at least the story behind it. I could see movement across the street, someone moving. Someone wearing red; red converse, striding the pavement like a gazelle from an aerial view. The runner looks back at the flashing strobes of the emergency vehicles, traveling on instinct, observing the slightest change in the herd around the crime scene, the runner zigzags across the road.

I move toward the door and open it slowly, peeking out as if I were hiding from something. It seemed quiet enough. I made my way to the lobby. I see Todd behind the front desk. He looks up from whatever it is that a hotel concierge does and smiled.

"How you doin' this crazy evenun?"

"I'm fine I just don't know about my unlucky neighbor."

"Yeah, they were real unlucky, like dead unlucky." Todd said raising his eyebrows giving a surprised expression.

"It's time to get out of Flora."

"Aw you cain't leave yet Miss Allyn, though someone gettin' killed down the hall would certainly give you somethin' to think about."

"Something to think about? Todd it's too creepy."

"Yeah, somethin' to think about." He repeated.

"Who was it?" I lowered my voice.

"All I know is it whatn' a guest, it was somebody that worked here, usually durin' the day. A day shift person."

I could see the nervous tension in Todd's jaw; he grinds his teeth each time he pauses between words, the lower corner of his face tightens and bulges out.

"I don't know too many day-shift people." Todd continued.

The sun was beginning to set and I could see a bronze haze cloaking the top of the city's architecture. The police were walking back and forth in front of the Regency doors. I couldn't figure out if they were protecting, guarding or just stalling until they got off duty. I'm sure someone from the police will want to question everyone on my floor.

Todd leaned forward and whispers, "I think it mustah' been that girl clerk. She comes in the morning. She comes on before me. She got this different color hair and these real long nails. I've only seen her, a couple of times."

"What was she doing on the third floor?" I asked.

"Ah don' know," he said backing up.

"Well, do you know anyone that wears red converse?"

"Red converse? What does that—?"

"Nina, Nina!" a voice called. It was Harper coming in through revolving doors.

"Hey, Harp, I see you got past all the excitement."

"Yeah." He said looking first at Todd then at me.

"Whoever it was died on my floor."

"They're dead?" Harper asked.

"I don't know for sure, no one has said, as of yet. I guess they're alive. I mean it was an ambulance not the coroner." I felt silly for making so much of the incident without knowing the facts. It was at that moment the doors to the hotel moved like a carousel throwing off riders; a few policemen stumbled in.

"We needs' tah' get statements from everyone that roomed on the third floor; third floor in the left wing." The first policemen announced. He stood looking as if he were blind and on a street corner yelling out unintelligible words to the passing crowd. Todd broke off from our conversation to acknowledge the policemen though they had not acknowledged him.

"Yes, yes sir I can get that information for you. Just lemme' get a print out of the occupants." The other policemen joined the first in a huddle around Todd and his computer. I overheard one of them say, "Smith, Green, okay, Allyn no, we don't need to talk to her. She wouldn't be of any use." Then another spoke, "What if she heard or saw something?" The third said, "Her room was half way down the hall. The others were on either side of the victim's room." The first spoke again, "Let's just ask her, and get it out the way. It probably won't add up to nothin'." Todd was showing all his teeth and colors.

"She's right here if you'd like to get started."

I pretended to be focused on the conversation with Harper, "So Harp how'd the meeting go…I was thinking about going over to the records office to do some research."

"Miss Allyn we need to ask you a few questions." The officer sounded half interested.

"Sure, what can I do for Flora's finest?" I said. Harper gave me an odd stare.

"Mam did ya hear anythang or see anythang that seemed out of the ordinarayyy, you know, strange like?"

"No. I just saw the paramedics rushing someone out."

"Okay, well thanks, we didn't think you'd know anythang, seein' where your room was located."

"Well, I did see something, now that I think about it. Someone running; running toward the lot across the street. They were wearing red converse."

"And what time was this?"

"This was right after they loaded the ambulance."

"Just someone running across the street?" The officer blinked his eyes slowly.

"Yes, and they were wearing red converse sneakers."

The officer took his hat off and scratched his head, "Why do you keep sayin' red converse sneakahs', as if I didn't hear you the first time?" There was a slight agitation in the officer's voice.

"Well, I thought it might be an important detail." I said.

"Oh, you thought it might be an important detail."

Before I could elaborate the revolving door of the Hotel began a slow turn, the chief pushed forth from humidity and heat of the languid streets.

The chief looked over our faces and summoned the officer to his side. Harper shouldered me, "Let's go."

I start thinking I really didn't want to stay in this hotel another night. "I don't think I can stay here, it's getting to be—"

"Well, if you need to, you can crash at my house. No room service though." Harper smiled.

I wave at the Chief as Harper and I made our exit. The 'whoosh' of the doors drown his voice to a muffled-garble. I could see his face, and his eyes were bulging and spit foamed in the corner of his mouth, as he expressed his desire for me to wait.

¥

We cross the parking area; I'm still seeing the Chief's face in my head, "Harp I'm telling you I saw some kid running in the same shoes." I start.

"Hey, I didn't say I didn't believe you." Harper looks surprised that I might doubt him.

I start walking away from the car. I decide I am going to see where the kid went.

"Nina where are you going? Nina, the cars right here." Harper declares.

I hear him come up behind me, "Nina what are you doing?" he said.

"I wanna see. I just want to see." I trot forward across the street into the lot.

"Damn Nina, watch the traffic!" Harper yells sounding out of breath.

"Hey where's this go?" I said, pointing to trail leading out of the lot into grassing trench.

"How the hell should I know? Well it looks like it might go up towards the highway."

"Awh, where's your sense of adventure Harper?"

"I'm not really dressed for hiking."

"Oh, please Harper you're always dressed for hiking, running, falling, sleeping." It felt good to laugh, too laugh like this.

We walk through grass, it cuts at our shins, creatures that were once lying still, move with deliberate speed to avoid our trespassing. The smell of the ground made me think of running; running with KK shouldering me in pace in the metropolitan parks back home. It was the anticipation of the trail or discovering a new turn off its path. I feel the same sensation walking with Harper; a tension of discovery, building with each stride into the glade. We could see a weathered pole-barn just ahead of us and my eagerness became a sugary treat on my tongue.

"Hey, Harper look over there. C'mon let's check inside."

"Nina, you sure you know what you're doin'?" He stopped, pausing with his hands on his hips looking at the rickety structure.

"Not completely, but what do we have to loose?" I said.

"There is a killer roaming free?" Harper started walking again.

"Okay you're right, but let's just peek in and go—that's all—just a quick look and go."

"Yeah, quick, real quick and go," Harper shook his head and kept moving toward the shed.

My hand trembled as I reached for the handle of the shed door. I wanted kick the door down and rush right in but I also wanted to wait and not hurry the experience.

I opened the door slowly. Harper pulled me back attempting to take the lead. I suppose he thought it chivalrous but I didn't need a knight, so I pushed him aside and entered first.

"Oo it stinks in here."

"Man, it does." Harper said.

"Look at this, can you see it? I got somethin'. It's one of those camping lamps, no kerosene smell. It's got a switch." I could feel the gritting residue around the base of the battery operated lamp and strangely the feeling on my fingers seem to get into my throat.

The light explodes over the tiny space revealing the intimate secrets the dark protected. "Whoa, what is all this stuff?" Harper took a panoramic spin of the room.

Heaven and hell have always been relative, rather than opposites; it's everything else that fabricates contrast, I thought scanning the old desk and stained papers, some yellow from age. There was a broken sign, broken in such away it took on the shape of an *L* or oddly enough a beaten seven, reminiscent of the tree Harper had shown me at the edge the city. The sign had once read the City of Flora, now one could only make out C--- - *H*ora. The *F* and *l* merged in a rusted blend. There were other signs for detours, speed limits and school crossings that lined the walls, leading the eye around the square footage, back to the desk where the city seal gave significance to ordinary paper as it rode the embossed text: City of Flora Transportation Department.

"Harper I know you feel something strange about what's going in Flora? You must, right?"

"Strange? It's insane and it isn't like this started yesterday. The odd thing is with the City Council and the murders that seem completely random…" I couldn't see Harper's face but I could sense him grimacing with each word.

"It's just about money."

"Hey, look at this."

"That's an old requisition, why is that something?" Harper leaned over to get a clearer view of the dirty paper.

"C'mon Harp put it together why would the city be buying this kind of stuff?"

"What, gravel and tar? Do you think they might have been filling pot holes?" Harper's sarcasm barely reached me.

"No, No look, look under here under *uniform*: 10 pair red converse."

"What?"

"Now, you still think I'm making the shoe thing up?"

"Truthfully I don't know what to think."

"How is this about money?"

"I don't know, but most things are."

"You mean you've never noticed anyone around here wearing red converse?"

"Not until now. I hadn't paid enough attention until, you know, wait I remember, damn, it'll come to me. I noticed someone—it'll come, I can't think of it right now but it'll come."

"We'll are you ready?" I said folding the invoice and placing it in my pocket.

"No, not yet I told you it would come to me."

"Harper, I meant are you ready to leave."

"Eh, yeah right."

It didn't take much time to get from the shed back to Harper's car and you could see a few people and police still milling around the hotel entrance. I had lost all interest in returning to the scene of the crime with my curiosity wrapped firmly around the folded paper in my back pocket. Then I began to think, why do I care? Let it go. Write the report and get back to DC.

"Nina, Nina, we're here." Harper's voice washed over my conflicted thoughts, easing me back to Flora. "C'mon, my mom won't bite. Well unless she has her teeth in."

"Eh, I can't believe you said that." I laughed imagining an old woman taking her teeth out of a jar, putting them in her mouth, and chasing me with the intentions of biting me in the ass.

The atrium resounds with a cackling pitch that seems to reverberate with a pendulum motion; voices peak and valley on electric sparks; weaving of news and soap opera happenings. The hallway opens up into a modest living room adorned with photos of loved ones past and present, framed by plaques and awards with Harper's name in calligraphy on some, engraved on others. There is a bookshelf with a variety of text, from high school Algebra to Dickens' "Great Expectations". The books outlined a fireplace that had not been used in years. There were round end tables and lamps with shades that appeared too big for the room with their dangling tassels that clashed in style amongst the floral prints and paisley upholstery. Blending in odd representation, two frail bodies swayed and surged at a blaring television setting on a wheeled cart.

"Hey, Mamadear, Miss Eda, this is Nina she's here from Washington. We'll be working together until she leaves.

"How are you young lady? Don't let these men folk run you ragged, darlin'."

"I'll try not to Mrs. Sims." I said sitting down on the adjacent love seat. I caught myself folding my hands and placing them in my lap while crossing my ankles and sitting without slouching.

"You wanna those police girls?" Eda asked leaning back and folding her arms across her chest.

"Oh, no mam, I work for the government." I said.

"Right chil' ah know, you one of them agents, like Holiday."

"Holiday, mam?"

"She means me." Harper said twitching his eyebrow, "I'll tell you later."

"Well, I investigate populations. I'm really, sorta like an accountant of people. I measure the growth of Cities and Towns." I answered.

"Is that what you do Holiday?" Eda said looking at Harper.

"Yeah, I guess that's one way to put it." Harper smiled at me.

The conversation ended abruptly when an episode of *Matlock* flickered across the nineteen inch Zenith screen. We sat in silence for the thirty minutes, plus commercials as Andy Griffith's *southern-hospitality lawyering how-dee-doo's* into courtroom victory. Then Eda stood fixing her dress then sweater.

"Ernestine, I'll see you tomorrow. Holiday, you take care boy, and it was wonderful to meet one of your friends. Such a pretty thing; you take care too, young lady. I'll see myself out."

"Holiday, I'm going up now. Eda call me so I'll know you got home safe!" Mrs. Sims bellowed. Eda had not quite shut the front door. You could hear a muffled, "Alright Ernestine."

"Mamadear, you need anything?" Harper helped his mother up from her seat.

"No, son I'm fine. Goodnight Ms. Allyn."

"Goodnight Mrs. Sims." I watched Harper walk her to the staircase that lead up to her room. A few moments later he returned with two beers in his hand.

"You hungry? I brought you a Guinness, until the *penne rustica* warms."

"Guinness Stout." I said looking at the brown bottle, "uh, no thanks but the pasta sounds good. Who taught you how to cook?"

"Can't cook, it's leftovers from Macaroni Grill. I got some cabernet sauvignon to go with dinner." He smiled.

After dinner we retreated from the dinning room to what was called in my house growing up the den, family room or television room. It was in total contrast to the small cluttered front room where his mother entertained.

"Wow Harper this is great room, 72 inch TV incorporated into the cd/dvd stereo system, surround sound, pool table, study area-desk and computer. Why doesn't you're mother watch her shows in here?"

"After my father died I had this backroom renovated just for that, but she said it was too unfamiliar. Like me father was never here, so I use it; another glass of wine?"

"Yeah, just one." I said.

"I've got some DVD's, you want to watch a movie?"

"Holiday and Ernestine." I said smiling, thinking the wine had kicked in. Harper said nothing at first. He seemed to be focused on his DVD selection.

"This is a great movie," he said placing the disk on the DVD tray.

"What is it?"

"The Killer."

"The Killer?"

"Yeah and hey lay off my mother's name, her great Aunt was named Ernestine," he said laughing.

"Okay, but Holiday?"

"My mother used to work for a white family, years ago and she had to be there day in and day out until she found out she was pregnant with me. She had to work all the way up until it was time for me come into the world and the day she went into labor was the day her employers gave her off. They gave her a holiday to have me. So my Dad nicknamed me Holiday. Okaaaay."

"Ahhh." I said thinking that was kind of cool.

Harper hurries over to the couch before the movie starts. He picks the remote up from the coffee table and pushes the movie select button. I watched the angle of his face curve and descend in the light of the room and it disappears; at least all that I have learned to recognize in the passing days fade into *want* of taste, smell, an urge, a decisive moment. And I kiss him. I thought it might have been the wine, but no it wasn't. I want to do this. I want.

I kiss him again, pushing him back against the couch, the leather grunts from the movement. I push him back with my mouth and tongue, inquiring, as I straddle his lap. I smile to myself when I heard the remote hit the floor. I reach back, pulling one shoe off at a time. I felt Harpers hand run up my thigh, caressing my hip until his fingers found their way under my shirt where he fingered my nipple into a delicate point. He pushed my shirt and bra up over my breast. I pull back from the kiss to breathe and his warm mouth encircles the tip of my breast and tonguing it rhythmically. It tickles a bit sending a small electrical sensation to my middle. I grab his head, letting my fingers feel his thick curls, which I tug with aggressive restraint. Harper rolls me to the side; his hand holds the back of my head. His free hand settles on my stomach where his palm burns my flesh with an excited tingle. He unfastens the button to my pants. I feel those slipping, pants and panties, passing the curves of my hips. Harpers face touches the inner part of my thigh. My legs tremble. Damn, his mouth is on my— his tongue, uh, no not yet, not yet. Back is arching. I can hold this, slide my hips away from his mouth. It's getting away from me. Whoa, there it is, shsssh, oh my goodness—it's out. My eyes are half open and my body is rocking on this peak. Harper is busy moving; his trousers and belt make a jingling-thud as they hit the floor. The couch burps as his knee pushes into the cushion. I inhale catching my scent and the smell of the lubricant on the condom. I keep my eyes closed and listen to sound of latex being rolled out with a rubbery snap. Harper breaths out shifting himself between my thighs and feel him push in me, warm and pulsing. I am still coming from the touch of his mouth between my legs and he slides into me intensifying my laughing inside; rhythm—there it is—uhuh—with each push I pull him deeper into me with the heels of my feet—yes—yeah—oo shhh. Harper stiffened, becoming rigid and tense, then he released, diminishing, like melting ice, falling from a snow-bank, collapsing, folding into my arms. My legs wrap around him holding him in me until each trembling wave fades into short breaths, then a cooing sigh. I swallow quickly, pressing my face into his neck. I didn't want Harper to see my mouth watering at the best 3 minutes I have had in over a year.

Harper held me tightly; he leaned up, looking me in my face smiling. He chuckles, "Wow, it's been a minute for me since I—"

I smile sitting up on my elbows, hardly noticing the belching couch and kiss him, "Yeah, me too."

He leaned down kissing me fully and I felt him all over again.

888

I remain silent, listening to the sounds of morning. I touched my between then with subtle certainty I cup my breast, hold it fully, then release it letting my palm brush over my nipple coming to rest. I thought of past lovers after KK, whom I loved far beyond the desert that had become the extent of my social interaction. Uncharming, Willard Finton, whom I loved for whatever reasons, perhaps one reason I loved him was that he came to me after KK's parting and college ended. Alone in a new world, first job; Willard knew everything, though middle-ranking, I was enthralled by his skill and for hours I would sit beside him in his office, in DC's downtown. I suppose I loved him as much as I loved KK even if a little differently. KK was stumbling through adolescents to adulthood and I was a part of his innocence lost, left behind until it became my turn at the tree of knowledge, taking the immense gift of life's authenticity. Authenticating, or validating ones existence always seems to be actuated by pain. Pain, I'd almost forgotten about Omahwali, his pain. No, I just refused to think about him. Born, David Barrett, he changed his name, he said for political reasons and dreadlocked his hair to honor his ancestry. He was Finton and KK all rolled into one; physically and intellectually. He was experienced but yet naïve because of his faith in the world's ability to change or rather accept him into its status quo.

I remember the last time we spoke. He'd just defended his dissertation at the University of Amsterdam. I remember the pride swelling up in his eyes, as he admired the signatures from the School of Cultural Analysis, scribbled across the bottom of his thesis cover page. He was so far away from anything American, Black American; yet he could claim the *golden ring*, fully on the merits of his *blackness*— on knowing his identity and imparting that *knowing* to academic testament, he was *their quested enigma* explained. He was the door for his academic community's search to comprehend the *Black* American. I was just along for the trip with a semester left for my Master's degree. I just wanted to see Holland and other parts of Europe; completion had not yet found me. But for him I was excited; it made me love him more, some how. We celebrated his triumph as if the world would end and then one afternoon he stopped laughing, "Nina. Don't you think we ought to go home?"

"Go home? What for? Let's go back to Paris for a few days."

"What are we doing here? I'm finished here. How long do you want to stay in this room, drinking and having sex?" He rose and came over to me. "Hey. I want go home. I want get married. Don't you want to start having babies; I want to buy a house so we can live someplace. Baby I want you. Nina, say yes. Why are we spending *couch time* over here?"

I recoiled, turning away as if he were a leper. I could feel him at my back standing, waiting, perfectly still.

"What is it Nina? What do you want?"

I didn't know what I wanted. I didn't know anything, except he had stopped laughing.

"I don't know."

"What does that mean?"

I turned to face him, slowly. "'O', have a little patience with me. Give me a little time."

"I want to, but sometimes you seem like you can go on like this forever. I can't reach where you are."

He began to grumble. I reached for him and held him. I had no revelation through his touch *what* I wanted. I let my lips encircle his; maybe tasting his air I would know what he apparently had discovered since the conferring of his degree. His body struggled to capture my rhythm, strained to find the familiar syncopation that so easily before entwined our embrace. I was falling or maybe ascending, evolving beyond his status quo, beyond his thirst to drink from the public watering hole. I wanted to leap, right out my skin, and leap in faith to something, that seemed, less frighteningly mediocre. Omahwali wanted to stroll passively into suburbia and from there the graveyard. I kept thinking, why open one door when you can open all three, I let the silence become judge and jury.

Omahwali's question hung in the air like ashes from a blaze that had consumed and devoured until there was nothing but the charred residuals of a lost civilization. The ashes settled into an immediate trip back to the United States. The flight was 11 hours and I must have watched the in-flight movies a dozen times on the small digital player. Omahwali didn't say a word, not even after the plane landed. We arrived at the baggage claim; he picked up his luggage, exited the terminal and caught a taxi.

I heard he is married now and has two children, a boy and a girl, living in Fairfax, Virginia, dread-free and quite plump. Sometimes I wonder if I could have managed the word 'yes,' how much of whom I have become would be lost to a *Stepford* life. Wow, I imagine those last moments on the plane he suffered terribly—the pain hidden beneath his face, mouth and eyes seemed to pull his insides. I could see it as he walked out of the airport terminal, pulling him down and away from me. He seemed to shrink with each step, not just in perspective but in spirit. He must have thought I was a real 'bitch'. I had no time then to be *thinking* what someone else might be *thinking* of me, no time, then or now.

But here I am. I wonder if Harper's mother would be waking up soon. This seemed so high school-like, having sex with someone in their parent's home. This made me think about the times with KK before he left for College. The exception being he was clueless regarding *lingua*, but the anxiety of someone's momma walking in on my naked behind while underneath or on top of their son is a sense of insecurity I'd rather avoid—the logic of after thought is easily corrected; there isn't any.

I could smell bacon, scrambled eggs and biscuits cooking. The smells had aroused smoothing in me; a beckoning home, an embrace, warm, familiar and inviting, and Harper's mother, the author of these aromas's aroused something different. I could feel panic, guilt and mostly embarrassment, scratching its way to the surface of my skin. If she realizes I'm still here, she may think I'm loose or worse, a whore.

"Hey, you hungry, c'mon let's get somethin' to eat."

I stood, moving in a robotic manner, holding my clothes crumpled against my chest.

"Now, you're shy? Harper laughs.

"Modest. I don't want your mother to see—see me leave."

"She made enough food for all of us."

"C'mon Harper get me outta' here."

Ω

We sat at IHOP, Harper reading the morning paper. A plate of unfinished chocolate chip pancakes with chocolate syrup sit with its freshness lost in the arid air of the restaurant.

"How can you eat that stuff? Don't answer that. Hey, listen, thanks. You know, for getting me out of your mother's house."

He looks over the newspaper smirking.

"I guess that means she's not going to see you, again, uh?" Harper's tone seemed duplicitous at best but the question was valid.

The waitress brought the check. I could only cheer her timely interruption in my mind. How should I respond? I don't know if she'll see me again.

"I got it." I reach in my pocket and pull out the requisition order for the red Converse All-Stars, crumpled in a couple of twenties and a ten dollar bill. The waitress sifts through the bills finding what she needs and I continue to stare at the requisition. The shoes had been ordered from Kline Sports. Chief Kline? It could be the same.

"Harper, does Chief Kline own a sporting good store?"

Harper lets the newspaper drop, making that paper sound when it folds.

"Yeah, he does. It's over on 5th."

"You think we can go by there after we leave here?"

"What about your report?"

"This will help. I think."

We enter Kline's Sports and the smell of new rubber and leather is overpowering. I feel my jaw clinch and I know now it's the cold air driving my skin into retreat leaving only a fleshy terrain of goose bumps. I had not felt the heat until we walked into the cool of the stores air conditioning.

"Hey Harper, how you?"

"Hey Mary Drew. I'm fine and you?"

Mary Drew is about 5'9" tall and 2 feet wide. Her hair is pulled back in a rough afro-puff, which she intermittently fingers for fluff. The polo shirt she donned rode up around her belly which protruded, almost with a force of its own revealing the metallic glint of her navel piercing. The left side of the blue polo read, *Kline's Sports* in script, while the name tag just underneath it read, *George.*

"George?" Harper laughs.

"You gotta' have a name tag. They never say whose name."

"Mary can you answer a few questions for this lady?" Harper signals me closer.

"Sure, I guess. Whadda' about?"

"Hi Mary, I'm Nina Allyn and I work for the government. I'd like to ask you some questions about this invoice." I pull the crumpled paper from my pocket and hand to her. Mary stares carefully at the invoice-requisition; examining it up and down, front and back. She makes thinking faces as her eyes shift around in their sockets.

"Yeah, I remember this. It was an order for the youth center. Mrs. Mildred's program; workers and volunteers wear uniforms."

"Okay, what else can you tell us?"

"Nothin' that I can think of."

"Okay, Mary thanks."

"Oh, no problem. Hey, um, I don't know if this is somethin' but they got an order that just come in. It's supposed to go over this afternoon."

"That is something. How's it delivered?"

"One of us; me or one of the other guys drives it over."

"Would it be a problem if we made the delivery for you?"

"Uh, I guess it be okay." Mary looked at Harper for some assurance.

"It's fine Mary. We'll get the delivery there no problem." Harper smiles exploding his charm, bombarding her senses, dismantling her doubt and leaving her a gesture of *yes*.

888

Harper returns to the car with a dolly and two adolescent boys.

"I brought help." Harper points at the open trunk of his car and the young men begin to unload the boxes; laughter erupts between them. Something about Harper's girlfriend being *fine;* my ego wanted to thank them but reason prevailed and considered they may not be talking about me.

"Welcome to Youth Excellence." A woman greets us, dressed in a bright red t-shirt, lettered with the three M's followed by this slogan: Midlred's Mighty Minds. We follow the two boys, carrying and pushing the boxes of shoes just short of the smiling woman.

"Thanks and how are you? Um, do you know what we should do with the shoes?" I ask.

"Fine, thank you. You can take them to the service counter; over there someone will help you there."

I notice the repetitive squeak of the dolly wheel as we approach the service desk. I feel like I'm in a tunnel, shrinking as Omahwali did. The difference is the world around him diminished in chorus with his psyche because the world, his world was an extension of his desire. It my world diverges, and disappears. I am landlocked perceptually; like watching the road again on the way to the last remaining tree of Flora.

We round a slight bend in the hall of the central area. I see a man with back facing us leaning on the edge of the service counter.

"Is this, excuse me sir, is this where we—."

The man straightens his red shirt and turns to face us.

"Todd?" I said.

"Well, Hey Miss Allyn it's nice to see you."

"You just work every where don't you?"

"It's the only way. If you want somethin' you got to be willing to give somethin'"

"I guess so. Tell me where do want the boxes?"

"You can leave 'em I'll take care of it. We got some new recruits comin' in and we gotta' get their uniforms ready."

"Oh, okay. Hey are there a lot of volunteers? I guess what I am really asking is: how many people have uniforms?

"Not many, for every group coming in a group is goin' out."

"Do you have a list I can look at?"

"Yeah, but why?" Todd gave a half grimace.

""It might help—."

"What, with the murder?"

"What makes you think—can I get the list?"

"Oh, yeah sure, um' here is the latest."

"Thanks, Todd. Hey Harp take a look at this?"

Harper reviews the list in a cursory manner, then his phone rings.

"Pardon me a second Nina."

"Miss Allyn you should come by the hotel I think you left some of your things."

"Oh okay. Are you sure?"

"Yeah, pretty sure."

Harper looks up from his phone and holds his finger up, "Nina… oh, oh, okay Mildred. Okay thanks. Nina that was Mildred, we should go they have some documents for you over at City Hall."

"Can you take me by the hotel? I need to see if I left anything."

"What is it?"

"I don't know. I never really looked through my things to see if I brought everything to your place. I kindah' left in a hurry."

"I can take you." Todd, watched the boys put boxes behind the counter", I've gotta' go in pretty soon."

"Really? What do think Harp? Can you pick up the papers from Mildred and meet at the hotel? You know I don't think Mildred likes me very much."

"I'll meet you there in an hour." Harper looks at Todd then me and repeats, "Give me about an hour."

888

"I climb into the crowded green Geo Prizm. It's filled with laundry and all the accessories: fabric-softener, liquid-soap, and dryer-sheets. His backseat is almost non-existent. The floor behind the driver's seat has several pair of red all-star converse and between the front seats 7eleven coffee cups and rolled quarters cluttered the space camouflaging the parking-break. The car struggles to a jerking start, and momentarily rolls forward on pure inertia then sparks, combusts and the road begins to pass beneath me.

"You know, Miss Allyn I to used dream of opening my own business." Todd spoke keeping his eyes on the road. His voice was different; lacking the effervescent energy of the desk clerk or youth center worker, but rather a somber, disillusioned man. "I had a complete plan. I even submitted my plan to the Chamber of Commerce. I went to Mildred, you know she's chair of the stipend committee for new entrepreneurs—." Then it happens. The quiet discontent simmers over into rage. "That dried prune told me my ideas were worthless and she would never authorize any deals of mine. She merely wants to keep all the wealth and opportunity for her self and cronies. An-an-an anah that wasn't the first time, no I don't give up easy, I kept goin' back and she kept denyin' me, but she, them, they'll have to start new businesses, when others start to fall apart. Things fall apart!" It was the first time Todd looked at me since we had been in the car. His eyes watered and tears streamed down his cheeks. "I'm smart! They'll see how smart. They already startin' to see how smart I really am!" He is laughing now. He looks over once again, this time removing his hand from the steering wheel. "They already startin' to see." His body shifts, his chest rises and descends. I can see his hand moving with the rhythm of his breathing. I am hypnotized, watching his hand, seeming to move in slow motion, becoming a fist; moving with the growing ferocity of his words. There is sharp pain at the bridge of my nose, I can briefly smell cologne then the pain shifts to the back my head. I can no longer see, everything is red; my head is pressed hard against the passenger window. I can taste blood. The side my face burns leaving my ear ringing. Todd's voice is growing muffled, I am drowning. The red turns to black and there is silence.

The rain beat the earth like a million hands on a million drums, calling spirits to guide the weary and the lost to a place beyond flesh, blood and water; beyond the moment but forever.

"We almost missed it! Harper Sims yells over the wet wind. "It hasn't rained like this in years," an officer standing in a barrage of scattered papers near the foot of the battered poplar tree shouts. He shakes his hand, flinging the water free then watches the lingering dribble from his slicker.

"Over here agent Sims!"

"Whadda' ya got?"

"They must have come here straight from the airport."

"Damn! We followed the directions. What's on those papers?"

The officer reaches down and picks a soggy letter. "This one is an invoice from the youth center for uniforms. This is—it looks like the case file. Yeah, here's your name. You were supposed to meet."

"I know. What's the paramedic saying?" A shadow moves gingerly around the base of the tree, pointing and gesturing. Another silhouette joins the paramedic, creating a glob of pitch that splits like a multiplying cell. The twin shape shifts and ebbs up the incline from the tree.

"The medics said it looks like a coma."

"Anything else?" Harper wipes the rain from his face.

"She had the crap kicked outta' her; it doesn't look good."

"Okay, get as much of this up to preserve for evidence and get her to the hospital."

The paramedic falls back into the gloom of the night, deluged in rain and wind only to be replaced outside the deep laminate of shadow by a drenched policeman.

"What do you think happened here?" The officer faces Harper, staring hard through the mist and streaming rain.

"Looks like a robbery, at least that's what the suspect claims as a motive. He picked her up passing himself off as a driver. But our witness, you know the kid with really red sneakers, said just before she got to the side-walk, when our guy grabbed her and forced her into his car."

"How reliable is your witness?"

"He said the victim fell at his feet, before forced into the car."

"Well, clearly our guy wanted to be caught."

"Yeah, he has a lot of knowledge about what's happening in this town."

"Nah, he just got lucky. Anybody could have been victim number eight; she just arrived at the wrong time, but the right time for him to make a statement."

"What the hell kind of statement is he trying to make, 'hello I'm a crazy killer?'"

"I know what you mean, but he's down at the station going on and on about social values being lost and women, especially black women not knowing their place anymore. And he swears this is just a taste of what's to come."

"I hope it's not too late." Harper looks up into the rain.

888

I open my eyes slowly, not because I am afraid, no, but my eyelids hurt from corner to crease. It is the contrary I feel, rage. It's almost as if Todd transferred all his hate and anger into me with each smack, punch and bash. My mouth is dry and there is this urge to clear my throat but something blocks the satisfying of this urge. I can feel myself squinting though my eyes remain closed. My head throbs with the luminance of light, warming the obverse of my face. No flesh or body seems to support me. I am a head bobbing up from the bottom of a barrel, like an apple in a child's Halloween game; treeless-apple, bodiless-head floating between the conscious deluge of being in the world and the unconscious inundation of being.

There's too much pain for me to be dead; that damn Todd. How could I be so stupid? Harper will count me missing when he arrives at the hotel and then he'll put it together.

"Mrs. Allyn. Mrs. Allyn can you hear me?"

Someone is calling me. I don't know the voice. It's not Todd's voice. I let the light of the room wash away indistinct corners and unfamiliar lines to a place more distorted to my sight than the blurred blindness.

"Thank god, she's coming out of it." A chubby black man leans over me. The light of the room is reflected off the thinning patch atop his head. I wonder if he is the doctor but his fingers are stubby and clammy as they grope my hand.

"Nina, sweetheart, thank goodness you're awake. You really had us worried."

The man gushing, a mixture of tears and gratefulness convinces me of the most overt truth he is not the doctor.

A lanky man is at my right. He has to bow and it makes him seem awkward and clumsy. Maybe he's the doctor? He's holding a small steno pad in a pink hand. His knuckles are white and they seem to pulsate as he clicks his pen habitually.

"Hello Mrs. Allyn I'm Harper Sims." The lanky man adjusted himself as he spoke.

Did he say his name is Harper Sims? I want to speak and contest but something is still blocking my throat. I taste plastic, it's a tube.

"Someone get the doctor she seems to be getting agitated." The chubby man rubbed my hand more intensely.

"Yes, right away Mr. Allyn."

"Call me Omahwali. I feel like we've been in this hospital the last couple of days together, formalities don't seem appropriate."

"Oh, well in that case call me Harper, um, but let me get the doctor."

Omahwali? What kind of drugs do they have me on?

"Hurry Harper, she seems like she is getting worse. Hold on honey the doctor will be here, just think about the girls and how much they miss you. They need their mom. We need you."

Who the hell is this and why is he talking to me as if he knows me? What girl's? I have daughters? Get this tube out of my mouth!

The lanky man returns with someone in a white coat. I guess it's the doctor. He looks me over, prodding, and poking me, shines a light in my eyes.

"It's good to see your eyes open, Mrs. Allyn. You gave everyone quite a scare. No, no, don't try to speak or move too much, you've been through a tremendous shock. If you're feeling any discomfort it's because your jaw has been broken and it had to be surgically wired. You suffered multiple fractures, wrist, rib, collar bone and your left index finger. We have you on a morphine drip to ease any discomfort, push this button." The doctor gives his best compassionate grin and hopeful eye contact and turns to the others. The men huddle together in conference; apparently deciding my fate.

It came to me here, as I lay awake, and everything slowed just as it did, before Todd struck me; ringing swells up, peeling away the layers of the reality swimming before me. A bell tolls inside my head nagging me attention, begging my will. I don't belong here; this is wrong; all wrong.

The three men gestured in a sluggish ballet in the middle of the reverberating room. I reach up to the morphine drip; with my good hand and I finger the plastic safety around the tubing. I can't be here. It's hard to find the path of truth or even in what is real in the midst of any life we lead, in this obsessive humdrum age of purpose blindness, with its architectural achievements, business ventures, politics, and its men! How could I fail to understand, the challenge of existence, not comprehending its aim or its pleasure? I cannot remain for long in either this place or the other. I can scarcely understand these faces, their words; their pleasures and joys that drive them to crowd around me, suffocating me amongst their variety of doing. I can not understand nor share in these joys, though they are within my grasp for which many others strive. Conversely, what happens to me in my uncommon moments of joy, what is bliss for me and life, delight and rapture, what the world universally pursues mainly in works of fiction; in a life I find absurd. And if in fact these men who seem pleased with so very little are right, and I am wrong, then I am insane. I am in truth the fiend off course finding neither home nor bliss nor substance in a world that is strange an incomprehensible.

So let me sleep and dream; live the dream, drifting down into the abyss; life rushing up about my neck, past my chin, mouth and nose. My ears immersed in garbled reality—I grip hard at the tube that holds me in the balance. The weight of my clutching hand eventually breaks the safety of the clasp that kept the morphine from following with liberty. Free now the narcotic speaks to my veins and I sink without struggle homeward; floating without restraint; I am—.

"I thought the good lord had called you home, Ms. Allyn." I welcomed Todd's voice along with the nausea that followed. Even here the pain tore through me like lightening across an expanse of sky. I am astounded by Todd's brutality, even more so if it is of my own mind. He slaps me again and I fall backward. I try reach out to brace myself my hands are bond. My back hits against something hard and knotted; everything becomes clear, blood in my mouth, pain in my back and Todd in the Youth Center t-shirt and red converse all-stars, standing over me. I lay underneath a bent tree with its crooked stance, in its silence acting as accomplice. Todd swayed back and forth blocking the sun with each swing.

"You can change everything." Todd stopped hitting me, leaning forward with his hands on his knees. "You can balance the scales. See, when you die everyone will have to stop and look at this place. I was meant to ride with you from the Youth Center. I was meant to meet you at the hotel. You was meant to find me and you did."

I tried to formulate a word but I only gurgled and drooled saliva and blood. What kind of imagination do I have? I die here or become the living dead there. My body was feeling heavy I can't move, so I watch Todd raise a massive piece of earth over his head, clutching it in orgasmic delight anticipating the culmination of his desire. He stops and his hands release the stone and it crashes into his on skull, toppling him off to the side like a bowling pin tumbling into the lane gutter. As his form lessens another rises in its place holding a broken fence post, the sharpened end up.

"Nina! Nina! You alright?"

Again I try to speak but only a garbled response is offered. The sun wraps around the figure like an aura of light. It's Harper; my beautiful Harper.

"My god Nina, don't talk. I think your jaw maybe broken. I'm so sorry I let you go with him. If one of the kids at the youth center hadn't seen you take this road I'm not sure I could have found you. We gotta' get you to a hospital."

I could feel myself slipping, traversing universes as the car cut through wet air, burning the ground with its tires. I was falling not just in and out of consciousness but with each descent I could sense the place where the men huddled and planned was very near.

"Stay with me Nina we're almost there. Stay with me."

888

The parking deck of the airport held the earth like some hollowed monolith too large for men to move so they burrowed through it to get to the other side; progress. But I doubt that progress. I sat on the deck peering out of Harpers' car watching the sun painted slabs of cement that represented humanities achievements. I stroked and adjusted my arm bundled gingerly in a sling. I guess I needed to be convinced of *where we had come and where we were going.*

Letting my eyes trail along the deck-opening they found Harper leaning, his back on the railing of the parking deck. I thought it was beautiful the way the sun worked its way in and out of his curls. I knew he was tired though he said nothing. I knew he wanted to tell me how he felt about everything. I knew by the way he would look over into the car every so often and weakly smile.

MILTON

Milton dropped to his knees, his hands held out from his sides, palms up. A blanket of silence cloaked the parking lot. He moved his lips, but no words sounded, leaving him an expression that told of something ill-omened. He slumped back, letting his haunches meet his heels and he sat. And, as if cued by an invisible string his head fell forward pulling his neck and shoulders down. His arms fell straight and he tilted, his face led and then his chest, as he fell and hit the ground. Milton lay fixed, unable to move. He could see shoes and ankles, cuffs and socks, moving back and forth, slowly. Someone even bent and gawked in his face, mouthing something.

***

It was another Sunday. Milton loved Sundays as much as anyone could love anything. He'd spent his entire life it seemed living for this one day. He got to church early this Sunday, as he did most Sundays to help arrange the music and offer any help in preparation for Sunday service. He stood, feeling about eight-feet tall in the choir-stand, fingering through sheet music taken from the piano bench.

"Deacon, Deacon?" He heard a voice calling; it bounced off the emptiness of the sanctuary.

Milton answered, still perusing the papers in his hand, "Yes."

"It's me, April…they told me you were in here getting ready for service…you directing the men's choir this morning?"

Milton smiled, looking up from his doings. "Yes, just trying to find a few alternate selections just in case our soloist gets cold feet."

"Oh okay…Deacon, I'd just like to say thanks…you know, for everybody in the youth fellowship and the school…and you know especially for me…for what you did for me."

"You don't have to thank me…if you young people weren't here, there would be no school…there'd be no Southern Baptist Academy. It would still be a dream of Pastor Claudia's. You young people and your parents made it possible."

"Yeah, but you really stood up for us…for me. I know it probably doesn't seem like much to you but Pastor Claudia can be tough sometimes." April was leaning on the arm of the first pew with her hands resting on her stomach.

"Well, she has her way." Milton said pausing, and gazing out past April, at the stain-glass windows at the back of the sanctuary.

"Deacon I don't mean to be disrespectful to Pastor Claudia…but she acts as if everything is either her way or no way."

"She only wants what's best." Milton responded moving down toward the first pew.

"She wants what's best for her…" April said sounding as if she were going to cry.

"Well you'd better get to Sunday school and let academy matters wait until Monday…you'll be there…right?"

"Yes…I'll be there." She said, turning and walking away. April reached the double doors, where she stopped, before pushing forward. She looked back at Milton, as if she was trying to see him more clearly at a distance. Then, she exited the wing. The door, pulled by some mechanism, slammed making a rumbling noise under the vaulted ceilings of the hallowed room—a place where people, calling themselves brothers and sisters, congregated in the name of worship—in the name of a common god. But really, it was a room for refugees, where souls were saved and love was professed, guided by an edifying assembly that sanctifies the dejected, through the phenomenon of shared spirit. How exquisite Sundays could taste, filling the mouth with god's word, washing it down deep in a person's soul, with the blood of communion and the tears of sinners. And here, nothing was to be feared, and there was no depravity of the human heart too great for those privileged to the anointing, who would lead that heart, any heart, to absolution.

Milton returned to the stack of songs, thinking about how the school had been started as an extension of the church—an extension of Sunday, making it everyday of the week, to help young people and to elevate their parents concerns about being exposed to the wrong influences.

"Good morning Milton, isn't it a blessed day?" Milton was sitting on one of the three steps leading up to the pulpit with his eyes closed, humming the melody of a hymn he'd chosen. He smiled, recognizing the voice.

"Yes it is…it's a beautiful morning, Pastor. I didn't hear you come in." Milton said.

"Actually, I was in my office finishing today's sermon and the spirit placed you on my heart."

"Truly. How so Pastor?" Milton said not showing much concern for the reason.

"Surely, you know it had something to do with Friday's events."

"Surely something good then." Milton felt confident, considering the topic. Claudia paused, while sitting across from him on the front row. Then, folding her hands in front of her, she established a proper and civil demeanor.

"Milton, was that April, brother Henry and Sister Edna's daughter?"

"Oh yes, she's a wonderful girl." Milton said noticing Claudia was already wearing her pastoral robes: royal blue with a pastel blue stole embroidered with her initials. The cuffs were in dazzling sequins that twinkled, stealing Milton's attention every so often. The hem correlates the style of sequins and because of Claudia's small stature it appeared as though she was walking on flickers of light when she moved.

"She's an embarrassment to everything I've done here. And you tried to use student and parent support at the expulsion meeting on Friday against god's will, my will…" Milton noticed her controlled agitation had now changed to open hostility.

"Pastor, Claudia, we all want the same thing, right?" Milton stood up.

"My school and my church must reflect proper values…and her presence demeans that." Claudia responded.

"Oh goodness, Claudia, she's a child, part of growing up is making mistakes, when did perfection become a criteria for God's love?"

"God can love you but around here you live by my rules!" As she spoke, Claudia's eyes seemed to catch fire, matching the glint of her robe.

"A single indiscretion shouldn't condemn a life, not from a place principled on love." Milton's eyes seem to plead more so than the sound of his voice.

"Tell me something Milton would you trade everyone in the *will*, for one person outside the *will*?"

"I don't know Claudia, what about the shepherd going after the one stray sheep?" He turned back to his search for music.

"Milton, as long as I am superintendent of the school, no one will bring sexual contraband into it. No one! What is expected of the students has been made perfectly clear to them and their parents and it should be clear to you."

"Claudia I thought this was a place of learning, didn't the Berlin wall fall?" Milton said attempting sarcasm, "C'mon Claudia you know she brought the condoms for an assignment in her social studies class." He continued.

"I've spoken with the teacher and learned that April could have chosen any number of other topics to cover for her assignment. But instead, she deliberately chose something that would reflect badly on the school and go against school policy." Claudia was standing and moving her arms about flashing like a glitter ball above a disco dance floor, as she spoke.

"Do you really believe she was out to hurt the school; that she really thought about it like that?" Milton said, loosening his tie.

"That's just it, she didn't think." Claudia said, as she spread her fingers and then made a fist.

"But April not ever being allowed on school property and the school being a part of the church, you take away her Sundays, you can't do that." Milton said, as he shook his head.

"You have the audacity to tell me what I can and can not do?" Claudia said. Then facing Milton and placing her hands on his shoulders, "You know, you're right, you are so right." She said squeezing the flesh of his upper arm. She stepped back, "We should finish preparing for service." She said calmly, as if nothing had ever transpired.

Service began and ended with the bliss of spiritual ecstasy; of song and dance, some call it praise and worship. Milton no longer thought of the conversation he had with Claudia. Even when she began her sermon, he was not reminded of the tiny angry woman but rather he could only hear the thunder of the anointed, hence the blessing of her words. As the spiritual storm subsided, those assembled under the ark of fellowship began to disband and seek the arks of their homes.

Claudia shook the hands of those that waited in line under the presumption that they could touch god on their way to exit, if they remained patient and smiled. Claudia smiled at Milton as he straightened the choir stand and gathered his things. Someone said to him, "Deacon, the men sure sounded good…that song…that last one really blessed my heart." The grateful man hugged Milton and then made his way out, passing the line to Claudia. She watched the man, then glanced over at Milton and clinched her jaw.

Milton moves, still greeting and being greeted, from the sanctuary to a small lounge. This was an area where people who were either handicap, or otherwise found it difficult to sit in the church pews, listened to the Sunday service. He noticed, as he passed by the couch and loveseat, that even the chairs were covered with plastic. He thought maybe it had always been this way, while letting the faces of the elderly, who often sit haphazardly around the room with walkers, canes, wheelchairs connected to oxygen tanks, fade from in his memory. He never noticed the furniture before, only the expressions of age; thinking that this is how it all ends, quiet suffering through faith and/ or affliction of Alzheimer and Parkinson's. This area had become a war zone and every Sunday morning a battle for the physical and mental condition of the elderly was waged. But mostly, the struggle was for the disposition of their souls; helping them to continue to love god, through incontinence, arthritis, and senility, and the general state of literally falling apart; helping them to realize god still loves them.

Milton entered the hall off the lounge that would lead him to the parking lot. He remembered something he'd overheard passing through the lounge area. Two women had been talking and one of them complained, "Wish ah could look at Pastor Claudia speak instead of just hearin' it, how come we stuck out here?" Then an usher had "*shushed*" them, as if they were children. He thought to himself, "Segregation in god's house: handicap to left, infants to the back, over 60 to the right, fat women to the alter; single men pray for a wife, outfits to cheap you can't fellowship, no college no salvation, independent thinkers excommunicated." Milton paused at the exit doors, wondering if this is what Sunday had become. Had the purity of worship evaporated under the heat of a political fire? Or maybe it too had always been this way and he was just too much a church elitist to embrace Sunday's reality, the reality of *everyday of the week,* which was personal policy-making for a select few.

Milton avoided this *wrecking ball* notion and stepped into the church parking lot. He waved at a few familiar faces. As he walked across the blacktop pavement, striped with diagonal yellow lines for parking cars, he saw April talking with her parents and a group of others standing by the narthex entrance of the building.

"Deacon! Deacon…you have minute." Someone called.

He looked back and April had run up to him, "Thank you again." She hugged him, letting her hand caress his mid and lower back. Milton, at first was put off by her affection, then ignored it as gratitude.

He moved, smiling, pleased that maybe the church is greater than it's politics. He heard laughter as he turned; then he felt something sharp strike him in the back like a bolt of lightening. It tingled for a moment. Milton dropped to his knees, his hands held out from his sides, palm up. Moving his head slightly he could see his reflection in a car parked near by and there was a soggy crimson rip in the back of his suit jacket. He could see April and one of her hands seem to glint like Claudia's robe. The glare flickered less like sequins but more like the steel of a cutting edge. A blanket of silence cloaked the parking lot. He moved his lips, but no words sounded, leaving him an expression that told of betrayal. He slumped back, letting his haunches meet his heels and sat. And then, as if cued by an invisible string, his head fell forward pulling his neck and shoulders down. His arms fell straight, and he tilted, his face led, then his chest, and he hit the ground. Milton lay fixed, unable to move. He could see shoes and ankles, cuffs and socks, moving back and forth, slowly and someone that appeared to be walking on flickers of light. Claudia bent and gawked in his face, mouthing, "You were right about the lost lamb, lost from paradise and the shepherd steers the lamb back—but just one, just one shepherd."

THE TELLING OF MICHAEL

The American Justice System is an organized insult to a whole people.

—Gandhi

A rushof flip-flop sandaled feet slide, drag and scrap across the cement floor, echoing like thousands of mouths shushing in an echoed syncopation, pursuing purpose without purpose. Muffled voices spring out of silence; rising and descending as the feet converge behind a cinder block wall, separating bunks and aisles of sleeping forms. A wall now pummeled and beaten with bodies of young men throwing one another against its surface in violent competition: who's *the real thug*. The sound of a fist crashing against someone's jaw; a man gurgles, as if throwing up under a thudding rhythm of slaps and punches and a body gives way to an airy moan. A pause, bridged with silence, ending with a disjunctive thump, then a rising swishing sound, slower, moving away from the back wall. I peered over from my top bunk; a crumpled frame lay still on the concrete floor, his head haloed in blood. It's 3:00 AM.

The morning's *early show at the fights* left me drifting in and out of sleep, unable to test reality or dream; like my days, no distinction from one to the next. Breakfast could easily be dinner and lunch, breakfast. Everything is the same from clothing to food. No change or break. The concept of "one long day" has manifested itself into existence; just being, no future or past only *now*. I find some solace in contemplating a spiritual design, providence giving a sense of purpose and understanding to my footing, after wading through anger, resentment and disappointment. But I finally came to terms with one reality—it began with me and it will end with me. I made these choices and elected to fight the system, behave recklessly as if there were no consequences, as if I were beyond the law— and for a time I was—beyond the law.

"Whah-whah-whah-it be like Doc B? Where you at dis' mornin'?" Malik barks across the aisle from his top-bunk, pulling out his earplugs. His face is youthful, not the countenance of a thirty-seven year old man who's been to prison three times. His beard and mustache trimmed neatly down to a thin line encircling his mouth then following his jaw line to his sideburns. He almost looks Chinese with his sloped eyes and yellow tinted skin, but the give-away, a front tooth framed in gold and the knotted corn-rows in his hair.

"I seent' chu' was awake but not movin'," he continues, "Whahchu' feel about today, Doc? I can feel the vibrations, look the trees is full, just the other day it was like I could see straight though the branches in the yard—it's go'n be momentous."

I smiled, thinking the seasons had changed and I had not noticed.

"THE YARD IS CLOSED UNTIL 8:30 AM, FOG ALERT!!" A voice crackles over the PA system. Then, "EeeEEERRRRWWOOOOOOOOOOO! This is a test of the Turnball-Correctional-Institution-Emergency-Alert-System. This is only a test. EeeEEERRRRWWOOOOOOOOOOO! This is a test of the Turnball-Correctional-Institution-Alert- System. This is only a test."

"Yep, sounds like somebody jumped the fence, again," Marvin Ambers said from a toothless mouth. He'd *been down* when a couple of inmates commandeered a truck from the warehouse and crashed it into the fence and then made a run for it. They gave up after about five hours, tired and hungry; they figured prison was a better alternative; at least you get three meals and place to sleep. Since the great escape, twice a week the alarm system is tested, and Ambers makes the same comment regarding the fence. I was curious about his teeth. His bunk was located next to mine, and I figured, close quarters, we've gotten to know one another, why not I'll ask?

"Mr. Ambers." I used the formal address because of the substantial age difference between us and too show respect. "What's goin' on with your teeth?" He laughed a toothless laugh, shaking his head.

"Man, I ordered mah' partials two years ago from dental, and they told me they was comin', but you know ah' go home in ten days." He lay back on his bunk, sticking his hand in his shorts, his face shrouded behind the hanging towels, draped from the top bunk like a canopy. This let me know the conversation had ended.

I grabbed my hand-made shower bag; a guy named Hill from B-dorm created it from the scraps of net laundry bags. The prison issues new bags to each inmate on entry, and when an inmate exits the old bag becomes Hill's sewing fabric. That was Hill's *hustle*, the *prison yard tailor*. He could make a complete outfit out of towels or convert them into bedspreads, blankets, carry bags or shorts you name it, for a few packs of *Newport* cigarettes.

"Another lovely day at Turnball Correctional," Malik said, tossing his bag over his shoulder.

The beating of *the white boy* at the back wall left its mark on the men, who barely moved when *chow* was called at 6:30 AM. Its mark could also be found swollen on the eye, lip and head of fates *less than authentic thug*, Harry Bender, A.K.A. *the white boy*, unlucky Harry. The thing is when grown-little boys, a true oxymoron, come to prison, pumped up on all the myths and gangsta' rap tales of prison life, they stay true to the badly written script: Arriving in this vast system of bureaucratic folly it is understood, according to *the Real Thug*, you must find a weak white boy and effectively *beat his ass*, and get thrown into the hole, thus you have successfully completed the first test of prison *real thug* 101. Poor Harry, he happened to be the white boy of choice and for the next month when inmates ventured by him their faces would contort to a lemon-taste expression followed by, "sheesh!" then hysterical laughter. But not everyone followed the real thug handbook, actually most inmates did not. Once acclimated into prison life: *You do yo' time, watch everyone and hear everything and never say nothin'.* That was the *O'schoos'* credo, and it worked. Clint Williams had mastered it. He hobbled his 6'4" gangly frame over to the chow line.

"They haven't taken you up top to medical yet?" I asked.

"Hell no and probably won't." Clint chuckled at his accusation because he knew it was true. "I bet I leave that basketball alone, now," his voice going up on the end, "I was playin' in the forty and over league—got me out here messin' 'round in some fake behind *Chuck Taylor's*, made by State Prison Industries. Damn near broke mah' ankle."

"Damn near broke yo' neck." Malik laughed.

"Sheesh, cain't even get a bratha' a crutch." Clint paused and looked at me, knowing I understood the comedy of it all and its tragedy. All we could do is laugh.

"So Doc, whahchu workin' on now, mane?" Malik loved slinging words around. Slang painted pictures with words. Malik, despised his birth name Ron, had been awarded a scholarship to State College for academics. He was a math whiz. What happened? I don't know, maybe too much of nothing. The smart, nerdy kid wanted to get the girl for a change, needed to be hip to get her, blah, blah, and blah. He lost his way like all of us.

"So what it is, Doc B, whazz goin' on fo' real?" Malik rotated his neck, snapping his head forward looking me dead on.

"Tryin' to get out," I reached into the pocket of the inmate made pants I wore to get a magazine clipping of the *Farside* depicting a flea on a dog's back holding a sign: *The end of the dog is coming.* Every single pair of these odd-cut khaki-slacks had holes in the pockets. The clip slid down my pant leg. I felt the scratchy edges of the paper rubbing against my thigh. Someone said the holes were there because the material is cheap, others say the holes are intentional so the inmates can masturbate. I just figured they were there so inmates could smuggle contraband. The shower appeared to be the area most commonly used for sexual expression. If you walk in at the wrong time and an inmate could be stretched out playing his own music. It's never wise to shower without the proper footwear because it's not the soap you might slip on.

A turquoise-green paint, not quite blue enough, peeled off the balustrade, separating the serving line from the main cafeteria. The strange color seemed to glow even in low light, against the frosting-white walls. We stood single file waiting for the day's concoction to be shoveled onto the plastic serving trays. A bright orange spoon and fork wrapped in brown butcher paper-napkins wait at the end of the line in a white tub beside the soup-can sized aluminum salt-n-pepper shakers.

"C'mon Professa' and get this breakfast of champions," Clint said. He and Malik were always trying to make me eat. The food was not my choice of even the worst cuisine. Oh, did I say cuisine? These meals were the closest thing to dog food I had ever eaten. So, I would eat to live not for culinary pleasure. Malik and Clint, stack chest-high helpings of the amalgamation on their plates, trading, bartering with other inmates on the *unknown*. I often think it must be fear or a pay off that keeps the Food and Drug Administration from interpreting the ingredients. Just imagine taking everything—and I mean everything—you have in your refrigerator and tossing it into a big pot then boiling it down and serving it everyday, three times a day.

We find a place in the corner, squeezing in and sitting on seats bolted to a small square table covered in brown Formica, which is also bolted to the floor. Ed "the mouth" DiGiantonio joins us completing the four-seat table. Ed sits down slowly, groaning out of pain and weariness. He walks the dirt track on the yard daily; now his feet are covered in blisters because his shoes are a size and a half to large, making movement agonizing. He stumbles slightly, bumping my arm, and I notice his olive skin, tanned to the point we share the same hue. His dusty blonde hair is combed neatly and fits a round face that appears to be held together by the gold-round-rimmed glasses. His stubby physique compensates his loss of balance as he eases onto the seat. I had gotten to know Ed after finding out through prison chatter he was a lawyer, thus the nickname "the mouth". We discussed my case at length, until I frustrated him. He told me in the most congenial terms that I was overly demanding.

"Goodmoring, Carol."

Ed was the only person that called me by my real name. I preferred 'Doc B' short for 'Doctor Black', Malik's idea or 'Professor', Clint's idea because I was always reading, writing or asking questions. I couldn't go by Carol because it was too *feminine* suggestive. So when I first got to prison I gave my middle name, Mathew to people that asked, until I got my prison nickname. I was so freaked out at first I went so far as not shaving or combing my hair for weeks just to keep from looking young and soft. I called my bum etiquette.

"Happy birthday, Mouth," I smirked.

"ED, thank you, Carol—but yeah thanks, how'd you guess?" He pushed his fork through something that may have been eggs.

"Because you look ol' as hell," Malik heckled.

"Your birth date is on your I.D. badge." I said.

"Counseeelllor it's yo' birthday, it's yo' birthday, it's yo' birthday," Malik chimed, while smashing the morning mush between two pieces of white bread.

"So what number you hit?" Clint asked.

"Fifty today, yep fifty."

"Well, here," I said, pulling the cartoon clipping out of my back pocket. "Happy Birthday, here's a gift from all of us to you." The table exploded with laughter.

"In our case the dog is biting the fleas." Ed grimaced.

"C'mon gentlemen, if you're done pick it up and dump!"

The C.O., Mr. E. bellowed, making his face swell, creating the illusion his bald brown shinny head was a monstrous boiled egg. If his shoulders and arms feel off he would look like humpty-dumpty with bifocal glasses. It seemed here everyone's imperfections showed, even the C.O.'s.

"Aw-here-you-go. It's too early in the mornin' for that, Professa'," Clint gave toothy grin, swigging the last of his milk.

"Well, Mouth, enjoy." I said standing, looking for Mr. E, "Hey, Malik are you goin'over to the school today?"

"Naw, Doc 'um on chill today,"

"Okay, I'm out."

I could see out of the corner of my eye a man named Street, stuffing slices of bread in plastic gloves then hoarding it in his shirt and socks. Some guys were always hungry. Alonzo Street moved quickly in front then behind me, falling into a bizarre zigzag pattern of walking. He came up beside me.

"Stay wit me, stay wit me."

I ignored him and kept moving through the central core. Street had so much food stuffed in his sock you would have thought he had a head growing out of his ankle. His belly already bulging screamed, *ridiculous* with his shirt ballooned with the plastic gloves of food.

"Mister Street!" Mr. E. demanded.

"Ah gotta' go now uh Mr. E., gotta go."

Street picked up his pace and you could hear the plastic moving under his prison tans.

"Streeeeet, empty it or take a ride to the hole!"

"Man wha, whaachu mean, ah ain't done nothin'! Ah ain't done nothin'!"

"Okay, Hotrod, let's go, let's go!" Mr. E. cornered street by the mirrored-window control booth. The C.O.'s sit in the booth and watch the inmates go by or they sit behind the one-way viewing glass and sleep without being seen.

I kept moving, opening the door to the dorm. A flood of noise and chaos drown Street's objections to be searched. The aisle leading to my bunk is at the end of a labyrinth of bunk beds. Bodies dart in front of me like objects on a computer game, forcing me to dodge the screaming shapes of men and boys. Senseless banter erupts from card and dice playing, while musty armpits wave in tempo to farting and belching in a symphony of flatulence. A final turn and I'm *home*, the thought nauseates me briefly, *my* bunk and 16"x24"x12" locker-box. Everything required to live is contained in the box, *Pandora's box, the black box*, this box that clutches *what is* my life: a towel, wash cloth, toothpaste, toothbrush, deodorant, a roll of toilet paper, a bowl with a lid, five pairs of underwear, four T-shirts, four pair of socks, two sets of prison tans, a paper-mate pen and a legal pad. I grab the pen and paper kicking the box under the bottom bunk and return to traversing the sea of pandemonium.

"Doc B!" A voice from the deafening ocean breaks its rising wave, and I turn siding in its direction.

"Hey, what's up Kenny?"

"Nothin', what's goin'on with you?"

"Same as yesterday and the day before that," I noticed Kenny wearing the bright orange state-issue knit-cap with a pair of huge headphones, "Just comin' off your walk?"

"Naw, Um' 'bout to start. Did you hear anything yet?"

I knew he was asking about my case. The *case*, I'm sick of the *case*, tired of the Judge. *Jane Bond* a wickedly sadistic, evil individual and a terrible practitioner of the law. Of course I would think this, she sent me to prison. I wanted to hate her but I didn't wish to give that much of myself to her *witchcraft*. Though Satan's mistress crushed my life by the fall of her gavel, I hold to a simple *truth*: One day she will be nothing more than corrupted flesh, a rotting corpse, dumped in some murky chasm and then what will this all matter? It won't. Or on a lighter note, I imagine her squatting on a toilet suffering from dysentery. Therein, sad as it may be lay my hopes. Inmates are always looking for hope, a *good* to happen to another inmate to inspire *hope*. But it rarely, if ever happened. This was *short-timers syndrome*. Time enough to ruin your life but not enough to forget your life.

The *short-timer* walks a thin line in prison. He represents the grace and injustice of an inefficient legal system. The grace is the length of *time* he or she will spend in prison. The injustice is *why* they are there at all.

Part of the tragedy is inmates with longer sentences do not embrace short-timers. Those with longer sentences are often malevolent toward short time inmates. I've been warned of brutal beatings and even death cause by resentment or envy of ones impending freedom. The State Prison system will, though it's not supposed to houses inmates with a few months with inmates doing ten or more years, possibly life, which can create an environment teeming with tension.

An inmate told me a *lifer* stabbed his short-timer *bunky* to death while the inmate slept, no doubt dreaming too loudly of his impending freedom. A lifer tossed his short-timer *cellmate* over the top tier to a crushing demise because his release date was near. I am a short-timer. Who am I to believe? Who do I want to believe? Everyone lied in prison so much so it made me never want to be dishonest again. *God* had abandoned *us* prisoners, leaving us to our own devices.

"Well, Kenny, the motion was filed April 15th and heard May 24th. The Judge didn't rule, but took arguments under advisement—so in essence she has done nothing but stretch this thing out."

"It's gonna' work out."

"Yeah, I guess."

"Man, I heard this guy Mike tellin' what happened to him—like how he got here and, uh how messed up the system is—he's ah real good dude—"

"When was this?"

"Um, just the other day, at one of the meetings I go to. You should talk to him," Kenny's eyes bulged as he spoke. "You should just talk to him, man it might help in your situation, or somethin'—um tellin'you he's ah' real good dude."

Kenny was always trying to be helpful; hopeful not just for the sake of the person he was helping but also for himself. He needed hope. We needed hope. Well, I did have my image of the dysentery Judge.

"I might just do that," I said, knowing I didn't have a clue what this guy even looked like, but I did enjoy *stories*. Listening to stories made time pass quickly.

"You know he writes and stuff too." Kenny adjusted his headphones and began walking as if he could walk himself free. I watched as he left me in a sunny blaze. It had rained the day before leaving a few puddles scattered around the grounds, but the sun waited out the clouds and prevailed in yellow radiance. Now, dangling just above the May blossoms, the sun insures its glimmer is not eclipsed again.

Injustice is atheism in action

—Pedro Arrupe

The sun slipped down behind the blooming foliage surrounding the barbed wire fence, surrounding the yard, surrounding the barn-like barracks called dorms that surrounded us. The penetrating heat cooled as the sun edged the tips of the trees near the dirt-warn path of the prison yard. I cut across the basketball court, trying to make my way back to the school building between game volleys.

"Doctor Beech," an even toned voice moved beside me. As I looked to my right I thought, I am 462203. This is who I am. No matter what I have done in life, every achievement, every honor, love interest, everything beautiful that I have come to know has all been erased by a single event.

"Hey, Mr. Hickman, going to the school?" Dave Hickman wore black-thick glasses, inset into horned-rimmed frames fixed on a narrow face, turning red from the sun, accentuating the gray of his clipped sideburns.

"Yeah, see what ol' Roose is up to today. I just finished building a computer game I call *Outpost*, and it's really kind of cool. It's all three dimensional imagery and animation…come over to my station if Mr. Roose can spare you today." Hickman laughed because he knew Mr. Roose always managed to find something for me to do. Not in a bad sense but Roose kept me around so we could talk and hang out; sometimes we talked for hours some days about everything and nothing. I mainly listened to stories about his family, friends and his youth, that *some how is gone.* He gave me free reign in the classroom and with the computer systems, most likely because he had no computer savvy, whatsoever. He often reminded me of my father though much whiter and balder. Roose and my father had similar views, both conservative and would bend if he took a liking to you, fussy, forgetful but sincere, as much as he could be unless under the scrutiny of the administration, and of course at that point, *your screw up is your own.* He continued to push and work though he was seventy.

"I'd like to see what you're working on, now that you have more time to play," I said smirking. "Hey, do you know some cat named Mike, he's supposed to be a writer or something in here?"

"Mike, that cat would be Mike Swiiih…" Hickman began in his computer style verbiage; "There he is right over there. He bunks right next to me…yeah he's a good guy." Hickman turned toward the school mid conversation, at least for me it was. I needed a few more questioned answered. *Knowledge* is power no matter where you are.

Moving in a strident motion, a short erect figure treads alone. His eyes straightforward, fixed concentrating, probably on the patchy ground of mud and broken blacktop. He moved with determination but without encumbrance. Every couple of strides someone stopped to greet him. He grinned and nodded, never lingering long, almost as if there had been no disturbance at all; then he started be back on course. I didn't want to be *one of those people* that choose to do time vicariously through another's deeds. Outside of the small circle of friends my curiosity wanes for the *story.* I heard rumors about Mike regarding his *case,* but I only knew the prison mythology not a face. I wanted to know how he carried *not knowing,* especially now, because he appeared to carry nothing at all; he walked as if he were Atlas, in strength and poise. He clearly was not the Titan of Greek myth, who suffered because he went against Zeus and was condemned to hold up the Heavens. Zeus' ruling had failed in Mike's case. He moved without the contention of the condemned but as if the Heavens held him up. He was muscular, like a college wrestler, about 5'6" carrying approximately 160 lbs. His brown hair is cut low on the sides and high above his ears, which bookend a boyish face compiled of ethnic features. An amalgamation of Germanic and Italian genes deepened by blue eyes that laughed when he did not. He was an immigrant; he was from somewhere else, some other place, not quite blending in with the prison landscape.

"Mike, right? Mike Swiger?" I didn't want to sound needy, not in prison.

"Yep, that would be me."

"Someone mentioned to me that you talked about your case the other day. I'd like to hear it, I mean if you're okay with it."

"You mean my testimony."

"Yeah, okay…" I stall trying to formulate a tactful question forcing my ego to go beyond the fact he corrected me. "So, someone told me you write too. What kind of stuff?" That wasn't the question I was thinking.

"Well, I've been trying to write murder mysteries with a Christian theme," he said, as the corners of his mouth turned up into smile.

"Why are you here…I mean what brought you to prison?" My eyebrows went up and my mind popped. The rumors that drifted my way like so much cigarette smoke billowing up, shifting in the airy rafters of the camp dorms, forced round by ceiling fans, until settling in the calm space of a drowsy morning, falling on sleepless ears, whispered murder.

"Murder…I was charged with murder," his eyes peering over me as if he were seeing something beyond the water tower, just behind the fence. "I didn't do it but…I was convicted as my brother's co-defendant." Mike said this to me as if it was supposed to sound better. Like he decided not to punch me with his bare knuckles but while wearing boxing gloves.

"That's kinda' of a trip, your case and you writing murder mysteries." I said attempting to be careful with my words.

"Yeah," he said, adding nothing for my mounting interest. It was almost like he was forcing me to ask. He volunteered nothing. I suppose it's second nature for an inmate not to volunteer information.

"You know I was taught if you want to write, write what you know," I said noticing we had looped the basketball court for the second time, "I've been taking notes on my experience in prison, trying to get a story out of it."

"Believe me there are a bunch of stories to tell."

"About a year ago, I wrote this story about a convict forced to choose between his divinity and his love for a woman. The irony, uh?… Given I'm a convict…there were some spiritual overtones throughout the narrative. But in my case divinity and the woman, well, spirituality is a karmic cycle, a kind of balance of positives and negatives for me… and the woman, she pretty much walked away from me when all this began. I lied to her once about my life and then this happens… "

"Yeah, I know what that's like I lied to my girlfriend too."

"You know once you screw up the trust it's a hard road to rebuild, I mean I thought we were on our way, you know, both professors, I was interested in her work, she was interested in mine…we touched on so many levels. I told her everything about me, not at first, but I did. She said I lied to her for nine months…*we'd just met*…but I did lie, building one lie to cover another, and she's relentless for the truth, then this crap happens and she believes it was just another thing I was keeping from her…"

"Yeah, I lied too, for eighteen months and now that I'm at the end of my term, I find out I might have to go out of state to serve twelve more months 'cause the crime crossed state lines. She behaves as if I held this information back from her; that I knew and didn't tell her."

The tête-à-tête of our relationship woes spills out like falling rain from swollen clouds. "Okay, I lied." I said, attempting to make peace with the loss of the woman I longed to see, "I told her my ex-wife was the nanny and my oldest son was my brother's and I lied about my age, but I also told her when I met her I was shady."

We laughed at the stupidity of it.

"…I mean that there were things about me that unless we were serious, like getting married or something she didn't need to know right away. I assured her it wasn't anything that would hinder or be dangerous to her well being." I babbled on, "I told her I had a terrible experience with a woman that I trusted and let into my space and she reeked havoc in my life for three years, and I wasn't going to bring that kind of drama into my family circle. Chloe, tried to forgive me, after we broke up, then we sorta' got back together, then this happens. She called a couple of times. I wrote a couple of times but…"

"Well, I didn't tell Sue about my brother beating his best friend to death, imagine that."

I let the words *beating* and *death* go through me, letting them fall to the ground in unannounced pieces. "Yeah, Chloe is beautiful but mean too, hard to let stuff go. If I was late I was guilty. Man, I miss her!"

"She sounds like Sue, ah' serious anger problem. I used to tell her she was *as mean as a snake,* but she was my snake." We joined in the momentary pleasure of high spirits, amused at our willingness to love with *always* good intentions leading to inattentive ends; we see a commonness that binds.

"Chloe's a brilliant woman, went to some of the best schools in the country, of course she would say, *the best*…has her PhD, well, she was trying to complete her dissertation when all this happened." I looked down at the muddy track, stepping around the swamp-like recesses of soil.

"Yep, Sue went to Case Western, did well in school, got her Master's, yeah, yep, now everything I do is suspect *since then*, and I'm in prison. We broke up for three years over the stuff with my brother…"

"So what happened?"

"We got back together."

"I mean with your brother?"

"Hey Bach, you comin' over this afternoon?" Roose stood in the door of the school yelling my name incorrectly. Mike was already standing with his hand extended.

"Well…" he said.

"Oh yeah, I'm Carol." I realized I hadn't introduced myself.

"Well Carol, I really enjoyed talking with you, maybe we can get together later today?"

"Hey Bach, when you get finished I got somethin' I want you to do," Roose said adjusting his black suspenders and turning awkwardly, letting the door slam behind him.

"Yeah, that sounds good, I'll be in the school until four o'clock count," I said moving backwards up the sidewalk to the school. I turned away feeling the weight of *prison* surrounding me and the *not knowing* returned, pushing at the back of my mind. My stomach pinched as my thoughts touched lightly on memories of my former life; an aching for home. Then I settle on Mike and he oddly felt like home.

I entered the classroom after a couple of minutes; Hickman labored diligently at his station, earning his twenty dollars a month. The AutoCad students worked with quiet ambition, whether that was for the *good days* they earned to reduce their sentence or the idea of learning a skill. And there was Roose sound asleep; his elbows on the drafting table, pen in one hand and a ruler in the other. I smiled thinking of all the spit and venom he could put out, protesting in a no nonsense manner, only to be pacified to a gentle spirit at rest, giving the last of his life to *us* and family; I knew he was a good man.

"I think I killed him," Hickman said.

"How's that?"

"Well, I told him I'd be leaving in about ten days."

"What? What's goin' on with that?" I asked.

"I'm transferring to a different camp. I need to complete a particular program before I can be paroled and this new camp offers it. When ya' gotta go, ya' gotta go."

The door burst open, Curtis Bell, the General Equivalency Diploma Instructor (GED) teacher is ecstatic.

"Don, you gotta' see this! Don!"

"What's up Curtis?" Mr. Roose perks up, wiping the dribble from his mouth.

"Hey Beech, Don come out here." Mr. Bell turned back toward the front door, laughing hysterically. We all follow, wondering if he'd cracked from the monotony. I had never seen Bell so excited about anything in the camp; normally his practice is the same as Roose—let the inmates sign in and fall asleep. Only Roose wouldn't let his students leave. If they were late or didn't show up he would go over to the dorms and hunt them. Bell mastered indifference. He openly admitted the penal system and its educational curriculum is a scam. Most inmates on average did not complete high school, so while in prison classes are offered to prepare and proctor GED testing so they might attain their high school diploma or equivalent. Great, Inmates think! Though for months they attempt to get into the class, only to be continuously turned down, until the last six weeks of their sentence. It takes several months of preparation before the GED test can be given, according to the course guidelines. This leaves only enough time for the inmate to sign in for the course so that his signature can be submitted to the budgeting committee for purposes of funding, thus the program is funded but no one learns.

"Do you see that?" Bell chuckles. "Beech, Cireno's in your dorm… what the hell is going on over there?"

Cireno stood screaming or maybe singing while stripping his clothes off, flinging them from one side of the yard to the other. His jockey shorts found their way to the lightening rod atop A-dorm. The dingy briefs flapped triumphantly as the yard cheered at Cireno's emancipation. His naked form charged out into the yard, leaping into the air, arms spread, and feet out, splashing belly first into a mud puddle. He turned over, pantomiming the backstroke. He stood up, ankle deep in the dirty slush, rubbing sediment on his baldhead and face. He swings around in a pirouette, arching his arms above his head, stopping to face A-dorm, salutes his fluttering *drawhs*' then bends over with slow deliberateness and scoops a clump of mud. He pitches a strike at Sergeant Danage standing on the walkway of the dorm, yelling at him. Danage was an unscrupulous loud mouth. His life, as I understood it outside the prison was limited, like most of the staff working in the prison system. He is unmarried, lives with his mother and has no friends except his church affiliation, which had done nothing for his character. But he loved the thugs; well, he wanted to be one—tough, streetwise, dangerous and reckless. So he emulated their behavior. He enjoyed pitting inmate against inmate, favoring those who bowed to his ignorance. Oh, I mean authority. He loved a *good ass-kissin'*. Sergeant Danage was the type of black man that slaves would call a *house nigga'*. I guess Cireno had had enough or maybe the mud that splattered on Danage's white shirt was his way of paying homage.

Cireno fired off two more clumps, running across the yard, until he reached the baseball field where he ran the bases, guards jingling at his heels; evasive action, his naked feet veered from the diamond into the outfield pursued by a troop of staff and officers. He circled the compound once more, crossing the basketball court, stopping to collect a basketball; after catching his own rebound and trotting off the court, he takes a heralding leap, landing face down, ball in hand in the muddy pool. He rolls-over waiting, waiting, waiting then nails Danage in his potbelly. The ball bounces back into Cireno's mucky hands; he slung it again, knocking Danage on his black baldhead. Danage stumbled back, his eyes like a pig, small, black and emotionless. Whistles blow and the guards holler for everyone to get off the yard. The inmates clapped and screamed Cireno's name egging him on, as they moved in subtle defiance inside the dorms.

"The yard is closed! Lock it down!" a C.O. screamed.

I saluted the underwear and entered the dorm. Count ended, no one had escaped, and we lined up for chow. It was *store day* so be very few people ate in the chow hall, and the inmates jumped around like kids on Christmas, elated they didn't have to eat the prison food today. The inmates made *breaks*, a combination of *Ramen noodles, Summer sausage*, a hot *Chili pouch* with kidney beans or made pizzas, all cooked in the dorms with a microwave, washed down with a *Foxy*—mix of coffee, powdered fruit punch or tang, hot-water then ice and shake—a straight sugar rush. Nothing is ever wasted in prison. For example the top of a can would be used as a cutter to slice meat or cheese for *breaks*. This and a plastic fork are neatly stored inside a plastic bowl with its lid, which indecently is the cutting board. Let the festivities begin.

I collect my tray and look for a seat; Mike is sits alone. I couldn't tell whether he was pleased with the meal or not. He seemed programmed to eat at a certain place and time. I sat down in front of him.

"Caroool ," he said.

"Miiiike."

"Did you enjoy the show?" Mike grinned. His expression reminded me of what a five year old looks like the first time he or she learned a joke and got it.

"Show? Fiasco is more like it," I said, scanning my tray for the most palatable mass, thinking fiasco defines my Attorney's ability to practice law, between his filing the wrong motion and fear of Judge Bond; a blossom of incompetence.

"I heard he flipped because someone stole his shoes."

"I wondered why he was walking around in those mismatched espadrilles, you know, boat shoes." I gave up on finding something I could recognize on my plate.

"Blaze orange at that."

"Sheesh, one was marked a size ten and the other a thirteen; he wore a nine and a half, at least that was what somebody said. I knew he was in the hole for something because they packed everything up… what happened to his stuff?" I slid my tray to the side.

"Sometimes the inmates or guards who sort through your stuff *up top* help themselves. Guards take stuff home to their families and the inmates, well keep it or sell it. He must've had some nice shoes." A trace of melancholy tinged Mike's voice.

"Man, this place is crazy."

"Ay, this is prison."

"You know I went into the bathroom and, well you know, I was gonna' handle some business. Well, after lining the toilet seat with tissue I attempted to get comfortable. So, while I'm sitting there I look at the stall wall and there are boogers smeared up and down the surface. THAT doesn't make any sense to me!" I put my fingers to my lips as if I would throw up.

"Some of these guys are, well they don't know any better." Mike looks at his watch.

"I guess we better get outta' here before." My attention is pulled to the serving line. I'm amazed, shocked, horrified all at once. Behind the serving line, mind you this is where all the food that is distributed; a two hundred and fifty pound butt-crack is peering its hairy-crusty-ashy visage out at the cafeteria floor. It casually moves by hot trays and food dispensers.

"Do you see that?" Talking through my teeth.

"Maybe he dropped something on the floor."

"What, his belt?" I stood, picking up my tray walking to the trashcan.

"Hey, Carol I'm not working or studying, c'mon on by."

We entered the central core and a C.O. leaned on the mailbox used for kites too. A kite is a form inmate use to access the useless bureaucracy. The mail only runs five days a week. Inmates cannot send mail on Friday after 8:00 AM and will not receive mail on Saturdays. The post office still delivers and pick-ups on both of those days, but the prison is understaffed and can't afford to pay someone to sort mail or pick up mail from inside the prison. The central core is a place where all the halls of the prison converge. If you look straight up, the dome ceiling has a badly painted Seal of the State of Ohio.

"How you fellas' doin'?" Officer Shay turned from the mailbox sitting in front of a window that peers into the chow hall.

"Fine, sir," Mike said then turning back to me. "You know Shay used to be a cop in one the small townships around here." Mike opened the door to B-dorm, "He picked up some women in the police cruiser, and I guess they must have really liked each other because he pulled off the road and they got in the backseat to get their *funky on* and they got locked in the backseat and he couldn't get to his radio. They had to wait until someone came by to let them out. Well, needless to say he got fired and is working here."

"Mike, funky on?"

"That's a little *prison jive.*"

"Mike, prison jive?"

We came to the back row where inmates doing *bits* or as some inmates might say *bittin' fo' real*, sentences from ten to twenty-five years. Mike has *been down* fifteen.

"Have a seat," he pointed to the bunk covered in a blue-velour blanket. His space like all prison accommodations consisted of a four feet by six feet rectangle, separating his bed from his neighbor. In the back row there are no top bunks; seniority earned you a single in the suburbs—others called it *death row.*

"Hey, um Mike, finish telling me about your brother," I said, not looking at his face but observing the constitution of his mind by the organization of his 4ftx6ft rectangle.

Mike's face seemed to shrink, drifting back and away from me. It was as if I were looking down a *well*, pulling at him to retrieve his thoughts. He spoke slowly and thoughtfully, unlike the buzzing staccato when discussing politics. He a conservative and me a liberal, we bumped heads on Republican and Democrat policy. He was devoted to the idea of an existing morality, and I held firm that morality does not exist. He a staunch supporter of *pro-life* and myself committed to the individual autonomy of *pro-choice;* we were a pair. His very words inlayed with religious doctrine, combating my philosophical stance. His zeal did not dissipate but had quieted under my inquiry. He turned inward, pausing in remembrance of something long tossed away in the *well* of his mind.

"The sun was out." he said, "I remember it being bright, a sunny day…

> *The smell of fresh cut grass filtered through the rolled-down window with dusty pollen clinging on the sun-warmed air. He sat quietly in an odd silence, a stillness…a unique hush swallowed the interior of the car. He sat without ease inside a space distinct from the muted tall grass that beckoned him in wind play gestures—waving him away, telling him to go. He could not hear what the grass said, or the trees cried out; the silence would not let him. His ears had become cosmetic, a mere contrivance affecting his other senses. His neck itched under the collar and tie; tiny beads of sweat popped from his pores. He thought, **how long does it take to make an offer**. He reached for the radio but again the silence prevented him from acting. Two figures stood in the distance, close in size and stature, one slightly larger than the other. Both every bit of two hundred pounds; he glanced at his small delicate hands gripping the steering wheel. The silence swells, suffocating the short breaths coming through his nose. He closes his mouth, realizing his chin had dropped leaving his mouth open, because it happened. He squinted his eyes as if that would change what he was seeing. The two figures moved in an awkward ballet accompanied by natures'*

orchestra playing a summer breeze. Their bodies flailing
about: one strikes the other hard in a downward motion,
using something to pummel the smaller figure across
the head. The silence tightens and vibrates around him
then it shatters, fracturing the air at the start of the car's
engine…

"Hey man, you ready?" a tall gawky man paced nervously in front of Mike's bunk. His eyes sunk deep in his head, giving his face a gaunt expression canvassed by flesh so white it hinted at a shade of green.

Mike pulled up and out of the well. "Oh yeah…" he said, looking at the digital clock sitting beside the small television incased in a clear plastic frame. Clear plastic so nothing can be hidden in the workings of the over-priced technology. Inmates, if they are interested in having a television, must buy from the institution at prices double the cost of the same item if purchased on the outside."…give me about two minutes," Mike said nodding.

"It's cool man…I'm still hurtin' from last time," the anemic looking man said stretching his long noodle-like arm out. He turned to me. I was sitting at the edge of Mike's bunk.

"How's it goin' with you man?"

"I'm good."

"Me and the Big Dragoon here workout together." Mike interjected

"Let me get out the way then."

"We'll be done in an hour, where will you be?" Mike asked.

"I'll be on the yard or in the library."

I developed a habit of looking down at the ground while walking, watching my feet as they move one in front of the other. Considering, if these are my feet I know for a fact the shoes I'm wearing aren't mine. The state-issued shoes will ruin the arch of your foot over time, forcing you to scavenger or barter for a better pair, not only for shoes but clothes as well. Fortunately, short timers cared less about footwear and apparel. But some take it very seriously, competing for the sharpest crease in their prison tans and whitest sneakers and too, *who gets* the largest clothes box from home, who has the most money on their books, the most waves in his hair…strutting in peacock fashion for a group of men. Prison is full backward social behavior such as library theft. An inmate or inmates steals newspapers, books and magazines from the library though ninety-two percent of the inmate populace is illiterate or must use a dictionary to read the newspaper, which is written on a third grade reading level. The magazine pictures normally become pin-up-girl contraband for men who don't get mail or visits, a fantasy of having someone.

Surveying the floor for cracks to avoid stumbling, I giant-step over phlegm and cigarette butts. No sooner than I enter A-dorm an inmate runs up to me.

"I fell Beeech, had an accident," Costilla said fidgeting. He was a man of fifty or more standing in my path with a knot the size of a golf ball over his right eye; a gash in the center of his forehead ending over his left eye, already swollen shut. I could see bits of white under the split flesh. Blood streamed down into his good eye, causing him to blink incessantly, funneling the flow to the crease between his nose and cheek, down his chin and dripping on the floor.

"You need to see someone about that…" I stepped back letting the blood miss my shoe.

"Pray for me Beeeech, pray for me."

Everyone knew this was coming. Costilla got in everyone's business. Accused of stealing and snitching, he always had something to sell. *He was at* the new guys the moment they walked in the camp carrying their net bags stuffed with their belongings from Lorain. Lorain was *reception*. If you get arrested and sentenced in Ohio you were sent there to be processed—the processing plant for *the prison industrial complex.*

Lorain is a closed prison, maximum security. All movement is controlled. Inmates are locked down twenty-three hours a day. When meals are served you are marched to the chow hall in single file and forced to eat four piles of ground refuse in three minutes. Afterward you are marched back to your two man cell and whatever personality your bunky is asserting. Lorain is the shock, humiliation in the extreme. Recreation is scheduled six o'clock in the morning along with phone calls. Showers are twice a week while a C.O. watches and times you.

The prison systems seems to thrive on nudity—strip searches coming in to the prison, before and after visits and when leaving the prison: lift nut-sack up, bend over spread your cheeks, cough, open your mouth, lift your tongue—hallelujah—lift nut-sack up, bend over spread your cheeks, cough, open your mouth, lift your tongue—hallelujah! An inmate said, "I'd like to shoot a stankin' hard one right in the eye of the C.O. when dey is lookin' up ma' ars'!"

Coming to Turnball from Lorain is like stumbling on to an oasis in the desert. Until the Costilla types swarm you. They want to know what you need, what they can get for you; what they can *get you for*… and for Costilla it was under the guise of being a good Samaritan—a lover of God. He loved when the new guy had money for *store day* in order to give the new guy a list of items to buy, which would pay off his Samaritan kindness, his prison kindness. There were more preachers than pimps in prison; it is here you learn to stay away from preachers, fags and lifers.

I was thinking, why ask me to pray for him? I should be asking someone to pray for me, sheesh! Costilla spins off like a top snapped loose by a pulled string.

"Whasup playa?" Clint hobbles through the day room commotion.

"How's it goin' Clint?"

"C'mon an get this work out."

"Man, I work out."

"Naw c'mon get some real work."

Working out, eating, sleeping and smoking about eighty packs a day are pretty much standard inmate activities year after year after year. In the State of Ohio the Department of Rehabilitation and Corrections is an oxymoron. The system is merely a landed slave ship, a packing plant, and warehouse, barns of cattle used to fund the bankrupt economy of a dead industrial state. Summit County loses the rubber factories but gains in marketing flesh. The prison industrial complex consumes sixty percent of the state's budget—the proverbial cash cow. The state built too many prisons too fast. With plummeting crime rates, there weren't enough bodies for the beds, so economics forced the legislature to formulate a contingency to correct and fill this lack of production. They created laws that imprisoned offenders for misdemeanors and instead of stopping at fourth degree felonies, which by definition is a misdemeanor; they have manufactured fifth degree felonies. Most States will not send anyone to prison unless the defendant has greater than a year to serve. But in Ohio legislation for sixth degree felonies is being considered.

"Pull! C'mon Professa'!" Clint said, sounding off in drill sergeant vibrato.

"Man—I—think—you're—a—little—angry," I say between breaths, pulling my chin up, barely to the top of the bar. My stomach tightened and my arms and chest ached. Fifteen sets of fifteen pull-ups, dips and twenty-five push-ups per set. Clint is crazy.

"I gotta' take a break."

"What? G'on over there and getchu' some watah' and c'mon and gimme' three mo' sets."

"Right," I said hobbling like him over to the water.

"See, Ah gotcha' some nice cold watah' in na' jug. C'mon…thirty mo' sets." "Two more sets and I'm out."

A serrated line of light scores through the sky, like the motion of a whip just before it snaps back and releases the crack of its tail, thunder sounded behind the lick of radiant heaven.

"Looks like rain," I said with relief.

"It ain't rainin' yet. We got time."

A drop hit me on the cheek, forehead and shoulder. "Here it comes."

"You got off easy today. Tomorrow we doin' twenty-five sets."

Clint was talking and moving in a shamble jaunt across the yard. The rain fell hard and steady as if it would never stop. Inmates stood at the windows and doorways staring out at the deluged yard, each holding the expression of a child being punished. I cleaned up and changed, putting on one of my four t-shirts freshly washed, dried, folded and neatly placed on my bunk, courtesy of Tom-Tom; he does my laundry for a pack of *Newports* a month. I walked to the library passing the ice machine just escaping injury from a flyaway ping-pong ball, spiked off the table. I rounded the pool tables and exited the door making my way to the library.

The library is quiet and serene, though most of the publications were out-of-date—newspapers were months old, texts missing pages or scribbled in graffiti—reading FUCK THE POLICE, across the leafs of tolerant fiction along side the obsolete law books. It is one of the few places you could escape the noise of prison. Alonzo Street is not here but out in the rain; singing hymns, crying and laughing with his arms stretched to embrace the rain. He hovered in the library most days driving everyone away with manic outburst filled with scripture, curses and farting. No he hadn't been in the library since is release from the *hole*. He'd managed to work is his way there on more than one occasion. The most recent incident, Street confessed centered around his zeal for God. He considers himself of all things a religious aficionado. And it had become his spiritual mission to confront the false prophets and rebuke them. The Volunteer Chaplin, according to Street is not a man *called of God* and he must be brought down. It's true that Chaplin Howard doesn't prepare well for his sermons, mispronounces words and often makes up his own definitions to terms he is unsure of; repeats the same point at least twenty-five times in a twenty minute lecture. Further, any criticism is an attack on his character and calling, which he takes serious offense. *So, it's left up to Street to fix'em?*

Again it appeared *God* had abandoned *us* prisoners, leaving us to the guiles of the misinformed inmate and the heart inspired, educationally and spiritually limited Cleric.

Chaplin Howard is suffering from Muscular Dystrophy and it has limited him to the use a motorized wheelchair called the *Sonic Scooter*. It looks like a scooter for the most part. It has a t-bar steering column, attached to a single wheel in front, glossed over in a coat of maroon metallic-chip paint with a single-swivel seat. On the day of the assault, according to Street, Howard verbally abused him then ran him down with the scooter. Other accounts say Street cussed the Chaplin out, and when the Chaplin called for the guards Street stuck his foot in front of the scooter wheel and began screaming, "attempted vehicular homicide". Thus, he took a ride *up top* to isolation. The distinction between *up top* and where we reside is this: we our housed in a barn called an *honor camp*, which means there are no cells, no walls or lock doors. *Up top* at the main Institution they have walls, cells and lock-up.

Street has sixty days until he's released. What should matter accept finding a quiet place and waiting out the storm? A quiet place, the library, so unlike the dayroom where you can't hear the television because of the dominos, cards, and chess. I did mention chess game. Only in prison can a chess game sound like the final four or an argument outside the neighborhood liquor store over who's *putting in* on the drink.

I sat in the silence of the books, not reading but still; listening to my own thoughts without the accompaniment of someone screaming, yelping or repeating the words to a rap song as loud as they could, sided by someone reciting the bible.

My body ached as I browsed for books, knowing I'd memorized every title. But it didn't matter I was wrapped in the coolness of the room; in its peace—anointed by the torrential down pour and the off chance somewhere hidden within these books I could find an escape. If not through fiction then maybe an obscure citing buried in the creases of the law books.

I scanned the spines, reading, recognizing and pausing to embrace John Milton's, *Paradise Lost*. I gingerly open it and read:
Of Man's first disobedience, and the fruit
Of that forbidden tree, whose mortal taste
Brought death into the world, and all our woe,
With loss of Eden…

I thought of Chloe, my *Eden*, her orient eyes giving purpose when she smiles; my sons—my jewels and treasures of a waiting life. My grip slips off the book, letting it fall to the floor. A warmth surges to the back of my eyes, filling my cheeks. The sky ignites in a streaking brilliance; I clinch my fist and grit my teeth, as if I had been struck by lightening. Stricken by a burning bolt, electrifying every part of me—down to the most basic cellular level, down to colliding atoms—rending me open like the cherry tree in the backyard of my childhood home. So distant it can only be a memory; Eden may only be a memory. Shocked, I let myself fall into a chair, exhausted by the sensation of loss, realizing everything is gone.

"I figured I'd find you here." Mike said, entering almost with reverence to the solace.

I relaxed my jaw and ran my hand over my hair. Speech evaded me.

"So what's crackin' gee?" Mike eyeballed me looking very pleased with his latest ruin of *ghettoese*.

"Mike, it's hard to know what's real."

We sit and listen to the rain.

"I want to be angry but it makes it worse and furthermore it's pointless. I chose to fight this case but getting information in here is limited. I have no idea what's going on outside these walls. I rarely get mail, when I do it tells me nothing. I can't call anyone. The only number not blocked is my sister's, and she refuses my calls. I have mailed out instructions for filing motions that would help in this matter, but my attorney is working desperately to stay in the good graces of the court. I had no idea he was working as a court appointed and a paid attorney. He gets seven hundred dollars a head for his appointed cases and that's a nice piece of change for convincing someone to plea barging their lives away. Myself, on the other hand, I am a nuisance. I am a client that actually wants something instead of the McDonald's *french fry* fix. But I have become a causality of war, a causality of compromise. It seems I paid the counselor to fall asleep at the wheel in order to stay friendly with the Judge and Prosecutor to guarantee cases come his way; it's all a swap meet. I have no one. I haven't said anything or complained because if I do what little contact I have is cut off…by my family! My mother is busy running her business—too busy to read my letters. My sister is too busy with her family to help. My ex-wife can't help because she is limited, as is my brother. My Dad has written me off and so has Chloe. You'd think I was out there selling drugs, raping women…or somethin'. They treat me as if I murdered someone…screw 'em'…" I notice that I'm talking loud and fast, like Street.

"Hey, I didn't murder anyone, and I've been fighting for fifteen years." Mike's demeanor remains casual as he spoke.

"That's uplifting, at least you have a network. You can call home, call your girl."

"Well no, Sue and I broke-up, no more phone calls or visits, but I can call home, as a matter of fact one of my oldest friends is coming to see me tomorrow and my parents the day after."

"I didn't think I'd be here this long," I said calmly, staring out the window at the rain.

"Well, neither did I."

"Must you sound so, like, *hey it happens*."

"But it does happen, it's happened."

"No one is coming to see me, granted my mother wanted to come but I didn't want to go through the strip search." I pause feeling ridiculous for my outburst. "I really don't like talkin' about this with anyone, especially you considering how long you've been down and I have so little time left, no sense *cryin' the blues*, now."

"That's all right, you gotta' talktah' somebody, besides I'm almost done, five months here and twelve in Pennsylvania and its over."

"Yeah…over…sometimes it's hard, not knowing anything…I tried meditating or you might say prayer."

"How do you pray when you don't believe in God?"

"How do you pray, and you do?"

"Easily."

"Yeah right, when are you going to finish your story?" I sat back in the chair folding my arms, sinking into the sound of the rain.

"…about my brother? All right, I can do it now…" Mike spoke like someone in a hurry, rushing to get to something more important. "Well, where was I…um' after I saw my brother hit Butch…"

…he pulled the car round and the figures came into focus. The larger of the two gargantuan stood over the other. He pushed open the car door, struggling to free himself of the heaviness of gravity. His limbs and the door weighed a thousand pounds, sinking his movement to an aggravated crawl. The standing figure raises his foot and stomps at the head of the prostrate torso. Again he looks at his hands, small and delicate comparing himself to the scale of the happening. He is close enough to touch the frenzied man, his brother who steps and kicks-in the face and cranium of the downed man. He thinks: this wasn't a payoff, grabbing hold of the giant's shirt, pulling, and fighting the grimness of the immediate. His mouth is clenched shut but there is screaming in his head. He can't hold him; stop him. A glint of light flashes from the gun in his brother's hand, both foamed in blood, blinding… he looks away…down at the twisted face; blood, he lets go. The giant still marches on the trodden flesh, still, inert, seeping in quiet nothingness. It's hot; the giant shrinks turning to him; he is his brother, and Butch is

dead. His brother pointed, mouthing something, and he stepped forward as if caught under the spell of his brother. He bent robotically, noticing he is still wearing his tie; he reached for the legs of…he no longer knew who this was; what this was; his small hands; what they felt. His giant brother opened the hatchback of the car without letting the weight shift…

"Are you two Youngstown State students?" A white shirted C.O. stood in the doorway.

Mike cut himself off, "No, but how are you, Captain?"

"Mike? Heeey, I'm fine. There's going to be a college class in here." The large bodied woman, blinked her hazel-contact eyes, letting her words drop mid sentence. She came all the way in the library. She moved like heavy women do with an oppressive authority. The Captain tugged at her bleached-blonde close-cropped afro.

"Carol?" Her voice is gentle and girlish.

I glanced out the window then over my shoulder in disbelief. I gave the captain an intense gaze. "Yes." The word slipped out of my mouth, however it wasn't meant to tumble free.

"You don't recognize me?"

Her badge rested atop a breast the size of a standing dwarf and history fell into place; high school. Her face is still the cheerleader although the color of her eyes is alien but in league with the years of accumulated portliness that carries the schoolgirl countenance. She is a big'un'. Anita had smooth glossy jet-black skin, reflective of the Nubian aristocracy in her genealogy. She'd wear her hair in a *natural,* crowning her flawless African features extending to her slim and graceful form. But in this time, this place her face is still Afro-centric round but dressed in make-up altering a chocolate brown complexion into an ashen caramel. I thought of Toni Morrison's *The Bluest Eye,* "…A little black girl who wanted to rise up out of the pit of her blackness and see the world with blue eyes…" as Anita spoke freely and easily, relating warmth and tenderness not revealed at the library door. The girl, I remembered. The woman was a stranger, an oddity. I considered what she might think of me after all these years—thin build and a graying goatee and in prison. But I knew she would ask. If I haven't learned anything at all about women, I've learned they want *to know*.

"We went to high school together…right?" I said, testing my memory.

"What are you doing here?" She sounded like a mother.

"Failure to comply."

"You ran from the police?"

"No, just disagreed…but I was in my car and it was during a traffic stop."

"They sent you to prison for that?"

"Yep."

"Where'd this happen?"

"Summit County…Akron."

"That's Summit County for you. You know they're arresting people for not reporting for Jury Duty."

"You're lyin'."

"No, I'm serious."

"I bet that's Jane Bond's doing."

"Jane Bond…she's a different type person…she's your Judge?"

"My nightmare."

"How long?"

"Six months."

"When do you go home?"

"…about four weeks…" I cut my eyes over at Mike, thinking what is this: the third degree?

"That's good, so what are you doing now, I mean outside of here?" She continued.

"I teach at a college and do a little writing. I see you're a Captain… how long have you been in the system?"

"Twelve years…I was at Lucasville and a few other Southern Ohio prisons and worked my way here. Those Southern prisons…the people really have a slave mentality. But hey, I make thirty-three dollars and hour and…"

At that moment I was thinking, *cash cow.*

"What's the deal with the Ohio Prison System? I asked, shaking the word *cow* out of my head. Why are so many people being jailed when crime is suppose to be down by eleven percent?" Anita is huge I kept thinking. Sheesh. I wonder if Chloe has gained any weight?

"Uh-uh...no not..." my mouth again betrayed me.

"Did you want to say something?" Anita asked.

"No, no go right ahead...I was thinking out loud."

"The system has to keep itself going. I remember when the only people in prison would be murderers, rapist and child molesters, you know real killers. But now it's all drugs."

Mike could no longer resist. "Well, the system has to perpetuate itself. So the legislature, in its infinite wisdom invented fifth degree felonies in order to keep bodies in the beds. And when crime rates decline further, they'll institute sixth degree felonies. Govern Voinovich built all these prisons during the economic boom of the nineties and now that the penal system is bankrupting the state, do you think someone would have enough sense to say, Hey, crime is down, we can close some prisons and save millions."

"But what about the guards who will lose their jobs? Anita interlaced her fingers together, letting them rest across her bosom. "That will hurt the economy."

"No, it absolutely will not," Mike said. "State jobs are a net drain on the taxpayers."

"I pay, we pay taxes too." Anita's tone echoed shielding.

"Yeah, but your salary comes out of tax dollars already in the system. All you're doing is recycling the same dollars. Tax revenues only increase when new wealth is created, and that comes through private industry. So, until Ohio finds another industry prosecutors will keep over-indicting men in an ever-widening net in order to feed the system. The judges in Summit County alone, will sentence a defendant to the maximum consecutive sentence simply for exercising the constitutional right to a jury trial, it encourages plea bargains. How's that for justice?"

"A huge net—a trap." I interjected. "Ohio is one big speed trap...a net cast out to capture fish. The Ohio legislation is the net and Summit County is enforcement, casting out *the net* of broadly interpreted laws capturing men to feed a system that is shrinking from its grandeur to austerity."

"You both realize you're in prison…right?" Anita said smiling, her eyes flashing their plastic light.

"Excuse me, Cap'n," a C.O. cracks the library door. "Mike, I need to see you."

"Oh, okay, I'll see ya' Captain." Mike walks around Anita, sliding between chairs and tables.

"Well, Carol it was nice seeing you again…you know, not in here but I'm glad to see you." Anita smiled brightly and the colorful eyes danced with nostalgia.

"It was good to see you too."

Mike made his way to the door and Anita followed him out, leaving me with my thoughts. I wondered again, how Mike had endured fifteen years of prison and managed to maintain his sense of humor and tranquil disposition. The truth of the matter is everyone; even the staff is a little peculiar in here. But he seemed much like the boy next door, growing up Catholic in a small Ohio town. The solitary events of his life held nothing extraordinary but when those single happenings are corded together they become a string of pearls. He was a fiction, bigger than life.

Mike would chuckle, looking away shyly recalling the first time a girl kissed him. He was in elementary school playing army with one of his classmates. Boys in those early years rarely made any distinction between genders. But girls did. The girl told him she was a nurse and he was a wounded soldier. She in her nurse authority ordered him to close his eyes to take his medicine, then she planted a big wet one right on his mouth. He jumped up running and she behind him yelling, "don't tell I won't do it again".

After kisses were no longer the dreaded plague of *boy world* but rather the treasures of youthful adolescents and cars the measure of young prowess Mike advanced in the world of men. He got his driver's license and that same day he had is first accident. He drove his father's truck into a ditch trying to impress a friend with his skill of *coolness in motion* and backed into a ditch leaving the truck aimed at the sky like a rocket preparing for take off. Man and his cars. You know that didn't stop the boy and his love for wheels. He spent two years restoring a vintage Mercedes, with the blessing of the god of cars and his father he was *coolness in motion* at the prom.

Moments, unconscious-changing points in time, flickering about without order until we look behind us and carefully count our steps.

His mother told him once that God had marked him. The evidence was a quarter- sized hole at the base of his back, where God touched him, saving him from a life crippled by *spina bifida*. And it didn't matter what the kids said at the pool about the way he waddled or the perforation itself because he had been touched by God.

The door swings open and I draw my attention up from my hands on the table holding, stiffly to Milton's masterwork. Mike's face is flush. He sits down in silence but his mouth tensed preparing for something. You could never deduce if Mike was angry, disappointed or distressing by looking at his eyes. The blue hued oculars always shinned, sometimes mocking the moment with their idyllic expression. The telling came with the way he held his mouth. If he were disappointed the corners of his mouth dropped like bending petals held down by the profoundness of April showers, and in opposition—which is holy joy—a Cheshire cat-grin swelling across a youthful facade that under the onus of sadness becomes a sober line, sullen and hushed.

"What's up, Mike?"

His words shoot out like rapid gunfire.

"Slow down, man...slow down..."

"Rumor has it I made the paper today...the parole board has supposedly revoked my parole..." Mike's eye never wavered but his mouth looked like a flat line on a heart monitor.

I stood on the yard stripped to my waist, fighting the melancholy resting on my shoulders. I tried to let the sun's affection sooth the burden; bowing my head under the force of the beading heat, tingling down the valley nearest my spine, traveling the tracked of tattoos: the symbol of creation, heaven and earth coming together, an African Endinka symbol for eternal wisdom, the Hindu Veda for God, the Bengli script for Most High, Greek letters: βeta, εpsilon, ηu, αlpha for *Beautiful-Eternal-Nubian-Africa* cresting the Chinese Dao half filled in want of its feminine complement. Each needled into the tautness of the flesh ending at the slope of my back.

Raising my head I opened my mouth as if to scream, only to be muted by the impacting sounds of the yard; blinded by the incandescence of the heavens and tilted in spirit by the turning in earth's nature, I move with purpose across this desert, clearing away the remains of desolation. My shirt in hand I stop and grab hold to the pull-up bars and yank myself up ten times, letting myself drop—fall away. The slap of my feet hitting the ground echo 'Mike isn't leaving when you go'. I enter B-dorm stretching my shirt over my head. Inmates bustle about like shoppers at a Christmas sale. Chaos breaks out as an inmate is caught masturbating at the window near the C.O.'s desk. The female C.O. rushes at the inmate with two other guards, barking, "Put that thang' away…Ah don't want to see that thang'!"

I slip past the confusion and find Mike with a newspaper flinging the pages from left to right as if smacking someone's face.

"You plan on leaving some of the paper for the rest of us?" I said. "Listen to this…"

…Michael Pratt is asking the Ohio Parole board to reverse a decision to release Michael Swiger on parole January 2nd. Pratt is sending the board a letter requesting a full board hearing on the case; hoping to persuade authorities to keep Swiger in an Ohio prison.

Swiger, 36, has been in prison since his 1990 conviction of kidnapping with a gun specification and involuntary manslaughter in the slaying of Pratt's brother, Roger Pratt, who was known as "Butch", of Munhall, Pa.

Thursday marked the 16th anniversary of that murder. Swiger was sentenced to 21 to 53 years in prison and was granted a parole hearing in September 2002 during which he was given a projected release date of January 2, 2008.

However, the parole board, citing new information received in the case, granted him a new hearing in September 2003 and in October gave him a revised projected release date of January 2, 2005.

The board refused to divulge the nature of the information it received.

Pratt said he wants a meeting with the parole board to explain his family's position on the release date...

The newspaper rustled as Mike peeled off another page to find the next section that continued the article.

"Harold Gwin, this is the same guy I sent my letter to because he kept misprinting the facts. He kept calling me the killer...confusing me with my brother."

"Where'd you get the paper?"

"Mr. E."

"That was cool of Mr. E...for a minute there I thought you were gonna' flip."

"Yeah, well this is how I found out last time. It was in the paper and running on the television news stations...before I was notified by the prison or the parole board."

"Man, that's crazy..."

"I could hardly sleep last night..." Mike stared at the paper.

"What else does it say?"

...If the board turns down his request for a hearing, there is nothing the family can do to stop Swiger's release, Pratt said...

...Even if he gets out Jan. 2nd, Swiger won't be immediately free.

He will be sent to Pennsylvania to serve a one-to-five prison term for his role in an arson at a Greenville furniture store in 1988...

"Boy, Mike, you were busy in the eighties," I said half smiling.

...Linda J. Karlen, 51, was sentenced to seven to fifteen years for conspiracy to commit kidnapping and had to serve her entire maximum sentence.

She will also be sent to Pennsylvania to serve five to ten years for the Greenville furniture store arson.

Swiger's older brother, Edward, 38, is serving forty years to life for murder with a gun specification and kidnapping in Pratt's slaying.

He had been Pratt's roommate at Thiel College in Greenville, and authorities said Pratt was killed to keep him from telling authorities what he knew about the arson and a pair of burglaries in Greenville.

The elder Swiger won't be eligible for parole until 2029. He also faces seven to eighteen years in a Pennsylvania prison in the arson case, the Greenville burglaries and possession of implements of escape he had while being held in the Mercer County Jail in 1991.

Mike laid the newspaper down and leaned back on the bunk.

"Well, at least, they didn't name you as the killer." I said, picking the paper up. "They even mention something about your letter and accomplishments. Where is it?"

...Swiger, in an October 2003 letter to the *The Vindicator*, pointed out that Ohio law at the time of his offense required offenders to serve approximately only eight months for each year of sentence.

By that standard, he's already served his minimum sentence, he said. He's been imprisoned more than fourteen years and said in his letter that he has taken responsibility for his actions, stayed out of trouble and has tried to give back to society.

He's earned two associate degrees, a bachelor's degree in business, accumulated more than twenty-two thousand hours of community service and has written two novels during his incarceration...

"It isn't a great piece," I said. But they didn't try to over sensationalize it, making you *Satan* or pump you up as a pious victim. The article is kind of middle of the road. Almost, as if they were afraid to add all the melodrama and negativity, but still refused to say anything favorable about you. They just droned out the facts."

"Yeah, so, how's it goin' with your case?" Mike asked.

"I haven't really talked about my case lately, huh?"

"No, you haven't."

"The Judge denied the motion. I got a copy of the brief and the cases cited don't have anything to do with my case. They don't even support her opinion. Anyway, I got another attorney and he's filing an appeal outside of Judge Bond's jurisdiction."

"Well, well, well it looks like somebody's is out of place!" C.O. Bell, stood behind me weighing in at two hundred and eighty-five pounds of baldhead, atrophied muscle and overly nourished fat that jiggled as he walked; swinging his long arms like an ape. A College athlete turned prison-guard slash preacher.

There isn't much difference between inmates and guards in most cases, both types have shaved heads, tattoos, are loud, obnoxious and believe that reading the Bible makes a man an intellectual.

"Ya' know you don't belong in ma' dorm, right? Did ya' ask me cudja' come in?"

"No, but..."

"Get tah' gettin'!" Bell raised his tubular arm and pointed a sausage thick finger.

I stood, looking Bell in the eye and he avoided my gaze. This wasn't unusual; he's never made eye contact with me during any of our less than cordial conversations. I am not special in this matter; Bell gave an entire sermon a few Sundays ago and never once looked at his meager congregation. There is an odd arrangement regarding the interactions between African Americans; even when we love *one another* we hate *each other*.

C.O. Bell, with his blowhard demeanor did me a favor; count had just been called and I wouldn't have known without his interruption. Count-time came and went. The regiment of having to sit on one's bunk and be quantified moved through me with indifference. I rarely thought of the reasoning behind having to sit upright on my bunk after learning it's to make sure you hadn't been murdered since the last count.

I changed bunks recently. I moved from A1 to A2 making home, now, a bottom rack. Clint and Malik where on the other side of the dorm and they rarely visited. You'd think my new bunk was in Tibet. But, I had a new bunky, named Russell, one of the coolest *brathah's* in prison. He is so laid back he makes me feel like I'm asleep. Russell had a streak of white through the left side of his neatly cut fade. But, it didn't begin there; it started in his left eye, running through his eyebrow then to his head. He told me a woman doused him with chemicals and the streak is the result. Russell is one of the only people I have ever known to go on a blind date in prison. I am amazed at the women who build relationships with inmates purely from letters.

Through the workings of prison-life Russell obtained an address of a woman and began writing her and this led to calls and now visits. This becomes even more interesting after Russell tells me he has a woman he's been living with for several years. And, even in this there is yet one more woman that he began with before he transferred to this prison. Now, his visits must be strategically arranged.

Mail call is always an exciting, dramatic reading from *Days of Our Lives, staring Russell.* Whereas, I'll get an eccentric post-card from my sister, discussing her academic struggles, defending her dissertation or a much appreciated drawing from my nine year old son of *Blade* or some other superhero. Russell's stories inspire me to remain free of chaos and drama. They remind me of a time when those things were the fruits of my life; too many women, too many lives, and too many lies.

I stretch out and my body relaxes on the sponginess of the bunk bed, staring up at the wire-mesh, holding up the mattress of the top bunk, I momentarily muse over the unnecessary complexities of social convention and individual expression. Recalling, the absurdity of the infamous *traffic stop*, I attempt to push it back to a solitary place in my head and imagine my sons greeting me with smiles, hugs, and a million questions. But, its stupidity overwhelms the congeniality of the imagined moment. Again, I conjure a pleasantry, seeing myself back in my office getting organized for the school year. I begin to drift, catching myself; I reach for my headphones and plug into the radio, mounted to the above mesh. The jazz station plays Thelonius Monk's *Straight No Chaser* and the lights go out in the dorm.

Consciousness gives way to unconsciousness and sleep peels away the surrounding commotion of inmate laughter and conversation, submitting to the cadence of jazz improvisation. I begin to dream in sequence to the melodic pitch, as the blackness behind my eyelids wilts with brown and orange leaves, dripping from russet timber; *an autumn day in Ohio saturates residential streets, and me, coursing the winter expectant avenues in a new car, high-gloss-black Mitsubishi Eclipse. My ex-fiancé invited me for Thanksgiving dinner, and I arrive with a bottle of Cabernet Sauvignon. She answers the door in a long form-fitting dress. I'd almost forgotten how beautiful Robin is; raven hair and doll baby eyes. Lately, this had been hidden by constant debate. She greets me with a light kiss and I—follow—behind—her, stopping in the kitchen to uncork the wine. We casually joke, discussing nothing of importance. She escorts me to the dining room table; Melvin, her father is already seated, drinking Scotch, chasing it with Heineken. She waits on me, serving all four courses and finally sits to enjoy her meal. Her mother joins us, long enough to give a brief hello and retreats up to her room. Other family members drop by to eat and run; Robin's sister and a group of their cousins and friends gather to plan their evening of festivities. The assortment of women, travel to their perspective corners of the city to change clothes and accessories. Robin stays behind to clean up and to make me aware, she's going out tonight. While she is talking, Melvin continues pouring Scotch in a glass, he has so graciously prepared for me. He's drunk, and Robin is ready to go. She hated when he drank and disliked even more, when I indulged him. She pouts and storms out of the house. I—follow—behind—her, carrying the lowball glass filled with Scotch. I didn't want to appear uncongenial by refusing Melvin's hospitality. I'd already poured the first two drinks down the drain, while cleaning my plate in the kitchen.*

Robin stops at my car and points, like a little girl at a carnival, choosing a stuffed animal, "Let me drive your car". "No. Why don't you and I go out?" "You've been drinking." She looks at the glass in my hand. "No, I..." She turns and walks brusquely away. I attempt to follow, but she's in her car and pulling off. I sit the drink on the floor of the passenger side of my car, and pull off after her. But she's gone. I decide not to follow—behind—her this time, but go home.

The evening is calm, barely disturbed by Robin's agitation. I select a CD and put it in the player, readjusting the sound. I find my favorite song only to look up and see the approaching traffic; it's red. I slam on the breaks, just stopping short of the crosswalk. The drink spills on the floor and I push the glass under the seat. There is a Police Patty Wagon crossing the intersection; it pulls off to the side. I figured they were stopping to complete reports. The light changes and I make my turn and the police flag me down. I pull off to the side of the road and wait for the cop to reach my car window. My car reeks of Scotch and I'm already in less than good standing with the police department. I didn't leave the department on the best of terms; whatever the terms I should have left Robin, after finding out her Uncle was the Chief of Police.

I let my windows down trying to air out the smell of liquor.

"Good evening Officer, is there a problem?"

"You almost came through that light back there."

"Almost, but I didn't."

"Is your name Beech?"

"Yes."

"I've heard about you—license and registration please, then place your hands on the steering wheel." I observed his size and demeanor while handing him my information.

"Mr. Beech, have you been drinking." I think, here it comes.

I waited, anticipating where this thing might go. And he returns. I asked if everything was all right he said, "yeah, you're okay," giving my license back.

"Well, if everything is fine I'm going to go." He walked back to the wagon and I proceeded to pull off.

I get to my apartment and park in the carport. As I cross the parking area, thinking I'm glad to be home the police pull into my driveway with lights flashing. The officer jumps from the vehicle, yelling for me to get down. I laugh and ask him is he serious. He un-holsters his 9mm. I ask him is going shot me? I attempt to walk passed him and puts his gun up and grabs by the neck and arm slinging me across a car parked near the front door of my building. I began to threaten him with all the city statues he was abusing, by this several other officers had arrived and I could feel fists punching me in the side and voices telling me to shut-up. A final voice, the black cop from the traffic stop said, if I didn't shut-up he was going to use is mace. Needless to say I didn't shut-up. They dragged me down into the station house, blind, running eyes and nose. I couldn't see anything he'd *sprayed me directly in the face, less than an inch from the bridge of my nose. I could only hear their plan to charge me with everything they could think of.*

"Doc, man, you goin' na' breakfast?"

"Malik, uh-um, what time is it?"

"It's 6:30."

"What are they havin'?"

"Pancakes. What was you dreamin'? You was movin' and talkin' to yo' self."

"You know, some things always stay with us." I pulled myself off the bunk.

"I don't know what that means but, okay. Less go geh' some of them cakes."

I found Mike sitting on his bunk typing vigorously with his headphones snuggling around his ears. He looked like a bizarre bird; perched over, picking at the keys, tapping, tapping, and chipping away at an unsculpted thought.

I stand silently at the edge of the bunk. He knows I'm there. He always kept his senses keen no matter what he was focused on.

"Caroool." Mike said pulling the headphones free of their grip.

"What's up Mike?"

"Just tryin' to get this letter finished. But, if you want, we can go walk."

"Yeah."

The yard clamored with the usual sounds of curses; the metal of the baseball bat cracking against the leather side of a fly ball, grunts from inmates flinging their bodies about the workout bars.

"What's up Mike, don't ever see you on the yard!" Someone yelled.

"I guess you don't get out much." I said.

"Nope, I don't usually spend much time on the yard."

"Well, now that you're out here."

"So what's on your mind, Doctor Beech?"

"Man, I 'm losin' it. It comes in waves, you know the need to be outta' here."

"It's natural, especially knowing you'll be getting out soon, no matter the outcome of your appeal."

"Yeah, I guess your right. Man, I wish I could take you with me when I go. The world needs you; needs that peace you carry. I need that peace."

"Hey, I wish you could take me too."

"Tell me Mike, does God talk to you?"

"Yeah, through his word."

"No, I mean, I'm talkin' supernatural stuff, cornerstone moments."

"Miracles."

"Yes, bonifide miracles."

"If you consider surviving prison for fifteen years a miracle, yeah."

"How do you know it wasn't just dumb-luck that's kept you safe? It seemed like dumb-luck that got you here."

"Fifteen years is a long time to depend on luck."

"But it happens."

"No, it doesn't, God's grace happens, even when we don't *know*, even we don't care, his grace keeps us."

"Some of us Mike, not all of us."

"All of us, Carol."

"What about—?"

"What about what—people dying—children starving? It's all part of the plan."

"I suppose the fact you witnessed Butch's death was a part of plan too?"

"I met you didn't I? If none of that would have happened we wouldn't be here now. There are no coincidences or random events, everything is tied and linked directly to God."

"I don't know Mike, that's kind of —you need poverty to understand wealth, grief to understand joy, hate to understand love-type of madness."

"Why is that madness? You've considered the Yin and Yang, positive and negative, opposites to create balance. Imagine a God that is that balance, a God that is all things in perfect harmony of His own reflection. So unlike us, struggling to mirror the divinity within us, but incapable to be free of imperfection. But yet, so much like us through Christ, we are up held in love and grace."

"That was kinda' beautiful Mike but I don't know what that means. Or what it should mean—to anyone but you?"

A guard blows his whistle and we begin to move like dinosaurs towards extinction; slow deliberate movements to the dorms to be counted and tagged before mid-day chow. I fell back on my bunk putting my hands behind my head, not letting my mind settle on my dream. Trying not to hate everyone that had anything to do with my being here, trying not to hate myself. I made the choice, but why am I being punished to this extent. Okay, think of Mike. But no one died in my case, no one even came close. I just couldn't—I wouldn't lay down for the sleaze of the police.

Everyday that went by became another sunrise and sunset of disbelief. The men that chattered and ate beside me seemed more like fictions, rather than real people. They were figments, phantoms of my imagination that sooner or later would fade with the coming morning. These manifestations would be chased away by the daylight, edging through the blinds of my Asian-styled bedroom, caressing my face, seducing me free of sleep. Then I wake-up and the ghosts still haunt me and then I realize I am dead. I am a ghost as well. No one who is alive, no one I know can see me or hear me. And maybe Mike is here simply to lead me to the other side.

The fluorescent lights buzz on at 6:30 AM. Sergeant Danage bellows for everyone to get up and "wash yo' stinkin' behind". Make up your bunk and if you want to go back to sleep go ahead, just as long as you have completed the first two orders. Insane isn't? Make your bed to sleep in it. My goal is simply to survive the next couple months, then I'm free, well, released into another type of prison—my life.

The day blurs by with its usual commotion and at its end Mike and I meet on the rough field of dirt and stone.

"Well, Carol what will it be this evening?"

"Well, Mike I think today I want God to show proof of his existence."

"Okay, how do you suggest God do this?" Mike's eyebrows perked.

"I don't know but I don't want anymore doubt."

"Then just ask him to reveal himself."

"You know, I really believe love is the answer but it is also draining and many times the love given is not returned."

"Maybe love is being returned but just not in the way you want it."

"Whadda up Malik!"

Malik jogs past us in full athletic gear, working to off the winter pounds of lethargic fat.

"Sorry about that Mike, what did you say?"

"I said you are loved and that maybe it's your response to that love that's causing you to feel like you're not getting love back."

"Shouldn't you know whether or not you're loved?"

"Carol take the time to watch a person's actions and don't lean on so much of what they say."

"You know I dreamed of my case last night. I still can't get over the fact I'm in prison for violating probation for a traffic stop."

"Get over it."

"Bring it in!" A guard calls from the dorm door.

"Well, until tomorrow." Mike extended his hand.

"Tomorrow, man."

We shook and the day ended.

Is it the next day or the same day? It's Tuesday or Sunday I don't know? But here's the yard and baseball field, scattered pockets of inmates discussing what? What could they possibly have to discuss? Escape? Revolt? What they used to be on the street.

Mike called across the yard, "Carol!"

We met halfway.

"I need a work-out partner today, you game?"

"What else do I have to do?"

He started by walking the yard and stopping at the cement base of a light pole and doing back dips. Then he would stand and walk to the next light and during the walks we would talk.

"You know I had this weird dream last night. I had just gotten out and on my way home. I picked up my friend Gordon and took him to my house, as I entered there was an old white woman cleaning my home. She seemed like an old teacher. Her hair was styled in a mushroom and she wore glasses. As we entered she said, your other friend is here, she curt and fussy. I went up to the kitchen and there washing dishes stood Chloe in a t-shirt pulled down to her waist.

"Hey beautiful, I've got someone with me."

Chloe pulled the t-shirt up, "I thought we were going to spend time together?"

She was angry and I could not explain my motivation for picking up my Gordon my first day back.

"Yeah, that is strange, the old women cleaning your house, really strange."

"Yep, crazy but I do see things in dreams sometimes."

"Hey, I've got to go in now and get ready for this meeting we can get back together at the end, if you want."

"Oh okay."

"Why don't you just come with me?"

"And do what?"

"Nothin' just come hang out."

The visiting room had been changed around a bit to accommodate the people gathering. As we entered we were greeted by faces from the outside.

"How are you? It's nice to have you with us." A young Hispanic man said.

"Hey, Mike good to see you again." An old man said, "Who's your friend?" He continued.

"This is my friend Carol."

"It's good to have you with us Carol. I want you to meet someone."

The old man waved a woman over that was in the middle a conversation with a small that had come in behind Mike and I.

"You just interrupted Phillip." The woman said in a curt fussy manner.

"This is my wife Helen and this Carol and friend of Mike's. He's going to join us this evening."

"Wonderful. Nice to meet you Carol."

She looked at me very hard, "Carol have ever attended any of our meetings?"

"No."

"You look very familiar to me"

"You look familiar too."

"Did you go to school out here?"

"No, did you teach school out here?"

"Yes, but I'm retired now—you sure I don't know you from some where?"

"I'm almost positive, but there is something. I don't know."

I turn away from Helen, almost in a panic searching for Mike. I find him in his usual state, calm and collected or as *Outkast* said, 'cooler than a polar bear's toenails'. He's laughing and talking Helen's husband. I can't wait.

"Excuse me, Mike I need to talk to you."

"Okay, you want to walk after the meeting?"

"I don't think I wait that long."

"What is it?"

"Do you recognize that woman?"

"Who, Helen?"

"Yeah, does she remind you of anything or anyone?"

"I don't know, should she?"

"My dream, man."

"Oh yeah, the old woman from your dream, that's right." Mike gave a hard grin.

"What? You don't think that's crazy?"

"I think God answers prayer."

"What?"

"You asked didn't you? Well there it is."

"What am I suppose to do with that?"

"Be thankful, some people never see anything."

"This is nuts, all of it. Man, I'm goin' to an island when this is over."

"Well, keep a place for me when you get there. C'mon they're about to start."

Tuesday June 10th 2004 they came for me. No, they come to take me home. They came to take me to court. I filed against the prison. I guess I got someone's attention. So, I'm packing up my stuff as if I'm leaving, but I know it's not my time. But here I go; here I am considering the law and its purpose or the *telos* in the *logos*, if you will. It happened while sitting in a courtroom with my ankles shackled together and my wrists chained to my waist, all this in response to a traffic stop. I am to be questioned with the expectation of articulating qualifying answers to respondent and for petitioner. But my mind falls here: If the law is in place to protect and uphold a moral ideology and further too reveal truth when it otherwise cannot be comprehended, why doesn't it work; thus deliberation within a deliberation.

I ask what the foundation of the law is. It is an understood supposition that morality is its rudiment. Now, firstly I have never taken to mind the idea of an existing morality, though it continually becomes a point of conversation and contemplation, with limited facts of its functioning existence. But with the aforementioned supposition I can infer that the law is merely a reflection of our moral state. And if that can be held as true the moral construct in which we exist must be flawed for the law in its practice and application is flawed.

Morality is the basis for a civilized society, a social construct held together by the *law* as an extension of those moral beliefs. But again if the law is the *hand of the moral body* it is failing in its social responsibility.

> For example: Two men stand before the same Judge (a thumb), one by definition of his behavioral history a deviant and an anti-social personality. The second man by definition of his behavioral history is an ethical component to society, a philanthropic personality. Each is being tried for the same crime. Both are found guilty and sentenced. The first is sentenced to community service and a period of probation. The second is sentenced to an aggregate term in prison.

If the example holds true what is the resolve? Could it be the nature of the crime or the definitions of punishment making deliberation inequitable and biased? The law implies that if act A is committed and B is the result then C qualifies as punishment. Simple, uh? Then why were the results in the example completely different? If the answer in the dilemma springs from the interpretation of the law, agreeing that if the law is subject to elucidation, then the law in itself being practical becomes impractical having value only for those who construe its purpose. But if the law is fundamentally prescribed from a moral derivation in which a definitive notion only exists as illumination, not clarification, then the law as subject should need no explanation.

Moreover the question reasserts itself: is morality a flawed proposition and can we ascertain from the former that morality does not exist? Then the presumption becomes plausible that there is no *existant*[1] morality to provide a schema as an archetype, which leaves the law, as variable and unpredictable and society emulating the erratic precepts.

If I were to accept the assertion that there is an existing morality as commencement then the fallacy is under the apprehension of men— and by result men are ill equipped to arbitrate *moral definition*, Man cannot interpret the law because he cannot comprehend morality. Thus the inference: men are immoral and cannot intellectualize the *moral question*.

It can be further argued that men choose to debate the law not due to it is moral err but more exactly that it is in the interest of the sophist (men) to obscure the issue of law. And that purpose leads not to a moral view but a skewed perspective of truth.

"Mr. Beech when you were ordered serve 90 days in the Oriana House were you free to come and go as you please?"

"No."

"Judge Bond's court argues that Mr. Beech was not restricted and could have left at anytime. The result being, his time at Oriana House was not confinement." The assistant attorney general interjected.

"As I was saying, Mr. Beech, could you leave without consequences?" My attorney continued.

"No."

The Judge added, "It seems we our attempting to prove whether or not Mr. Beech's participation in the Oriana House program can be considered as confinement instead of him being held unlawfully in Turnball County. I believe Judge Bond's court has already decided on the issue of confinement and if that is the argument today, Mr. Beech should file an appeal in Bond's jurisdiction."

---

1 Martin Hiedeggar, *Being in Time,*
existant-to be, it is

I knew at that point, though the supreme agreed that Oriana House qualified as confinement, this court would not rule against Bond's court. No, stepping on political toes. "What does this God want? I may not be innocent but I'm not guilty of what they say."

I could see Mike in my mind, waving at me as the van drove by the garden he tended for the battered women's shelter. Who was I, alone, shackled, police escort to an empty courtroom. The room was filled with lawyers, a court reporter, the judge, the police and me. Who did I kill?

"Mr. Beech isn't true you will be released in ten days?" The assistant attorney general smirked as this question slithered out of his mouth, "I believe your release date is your birthday, am I correct?"

"Yes, but what—"

My Attorney looked at me with an 'oh well' expression.

It wasn't long after that I found myself back in the camp, explaining over and over again why I was packed up and shipped out. How much more absurd can the world be? I wonder if Mike is going to be okay when the time comes for him to leave.

I tapped the edge of Mike's bunk. It was about 7:31 AM.

"Mike hey, I gotta' go…they called for me…" I whispered.

Jokingly he said, "Man, um gonna' have to get ma' stick…you know I sleep in today."

"Hey I'm about to leave."

Mike looked at me as if saying *man um' gonna' see you later.* And I believed his eyes but the truth remained, today I leave. His bigger than life persona, like a character in a fiction dimmed. His eyes clouded over like blue-sky overcast by a coming storm. I loved him, this small man, a convict an inmate.

"Let's go Beech!" The C.O. called.

He reached up holding my hand, "God has you."

I looked at him hard experiencing the awkwardness of the moment letting his hand go I walked away; moving in and through A-dorm, partly hearing the good lucks, barely acknowledging goodbyes. I gathered my papers and bagged the state blankets and prison clothes, dumping them in a bin at the quartermaster's door. A guard waited just to escort me out. I realized this could be the last I'd ever see of Mike. I thought of him with disbelief; our journey is ending. He is an immigrant; a foreigner. He is *God's own.*

Epilogue

Ed DiGiantonio died twenty days before his release. He'd served eleventh months on twelve month bit. Clint returned to the old neighborhood, trying make up for lost time, after nine months donated to the system in free labor and just simply occupying space for the states accounting purposes, *once again it was own*. He understood the system. He just couldn't get caught again.

Malik was relased 18 months later on PRC post release control for two years. Kenny was paroled as well, also on PRC for three years. If either were to violate the conditions of their PRC he could be sent back to prison for up to nine months, plus the remainder of his sentence. A violation could be as simple a parking ticket.

The camp closed about a year ago and all remaining inmates were scattered across the state. There has been a rise in female offenders according the State of Ohio and they need the Turnball facility to house these women; it appears *the corporation* is expanding its product base.

Mike finally made it to Pennsylvania to complete the remaining months of his sentence. He was paroled to Cuyahoga County where he and his love of fifteen years reside with their newborn. He is an associate pastor in prison ministry at one of the local churches. He writes often, maintaining his love of God and the Republicans. Me, well I got my Island. The smell of prison has all but faded by scented oils and bath-beads, washed over with fresh papaya and coconut. Island life agrees with me, though Chloe, with PhD. in hand, has been replaced by sun bathed native girls and ocean breezes. I am free, right?

Inaugural Blue

4.1.92

Dear Professor:

Today they gave me my gun. It was for some, a genuine transforming moment. You know the kind of moment you used to tell me about. A moment when a thing happens to a man and he changes, sometimes for the better and sometimes for the worst.

I swear this little guy, everyone calls Swanko, short for Swankovich, grew four inches as soon as the gun touched his hand. I guess guns have that effect on people. It was strange holding the gun (a gun) for the first time, its weight felt awkward in my hand. It's hard to believe that there is so much controversy, fear and death that surround the 51/2 pound steel mechanism—Smith & Wesson 5906, serial number E1406. They made us memorize this.

I tested at the level of Master Marksmen but I don't feel like I have achieved much. Swanko and the others were very excited.

Yours Truly,
Eli

4.9.92

Dear Professor:

I know I didn't inform you that I decided to take this job. I really hadn't made up my mind until I got the letter from the Mayor's office.

Out of 2000 applicants 400 were selected to take the test. And the top 50 were selected for psychological and physical testing. And from there 25 were selected to attend the Academy.

Well, aside from the chronology of how I got the job, I'm sure you're curious to know why I didn't inform you. I didn't tell you because I knew exactly what you would say. You would start by telling me that I am an adult free to do whatever I choose. And you would finish by telling me that African-Americans have a responsibility to their communities not to the state. And my becoming a Police Officer is a form of betrayal to the family, community and most of all myself. Police, for so long, have been an oppressive faction to African-American culture, why would I join the enemy's camp? 5 years of college and two Bachelors', 9 hours short of a Master Degree and I decide my education has no value. Nonetheless a job that only requires a high school education or its equivalent seems to satisfy my intellectual yearning. I know you would say something just like that.

You would never consider that I could be an intermediary between the system and the people in the community.

Your Son,
Eli

4.12.92

Dear Professor:

    I started a letter to Momma but I figured it would end up being a part of a Wednesday night prayer meeting or Sunday morning invocation. I know she loves me but everything isn't for the "threshing floor." I know she'll be praying for me. And her-self, because the subject of me *not* being a policeman is the only thing in 25 years you two have agreed on. I'm barely a cop and already I'm resolving domestic conflicts.

Your son,
Eli

4.21.92

Professor:

Roll call is something like high school homeroom. We actually have to sit in classroom type fashion, behind Ping-Pong paddle shaped desk. Someone in the back of the room farting and wisecracking under his breath. There's the dirty kid that never ties his shoes or tucks his shirt, let alone combs his hair. Then you have the cool one, Mr. Cool, he always wears his clothes slightly different and it works for him. Class is not complete without the nerd, or geek with his glasses and pocket protector. And then there are the girls. The one everyone wants and the one everyone claims they have had and finally the bully and his sidekick, the classes snitch. Imagine all this packaged in a police uniform. It makes for a strange comedy. They all seem to be good-hearted people. I mean they have to be they're the police.

At this particular roll call we were assigned to our field training officers (FTO) The shift Commander, an older man with glasses, no chin, no lips just a nose. A face of nose and glasses under a Ronald Reagan hair-do. He reminded me of a librarian.

He called everyone by name, last name first and if you did not answer properly with anything less than a boot camp bellow 'Here Sir!', he'd call you something I won't repeat. He's probably just trying to prepare everyone's mental state for the work that's ahead. Of course my FTO said the commander is a prick.

My FTO is a 25-year veteran, he's black and all he talks about is retirement. Last night was the first time I patrolled the streets. Otis, my FTO kept mentioning that I'd better not do anything that could jeopardize his pension.

I'll work from 11p.m. to 7a.m., so most of my letters I'll write at the end of shift. It will help me relax and sleep.

Your son,
Eli

4.30.92

Dear Professor:

Last night Otis and I patrolled the streets and everything moved at a lazy pace, slow and rehearsed. I felt like a ghost; a shadow silently moving through people's lives, watching their anguish. Their personal happenings which I stand over and judge. Otis reminds me never to get involved beyond the limits of the job. He asked me if I liked fishing. He loves it. I don't particularly care for fishing, as you know. You throw your line out and hope to catch something—gambling on the intelligence of fish.

Hey, one interesting thing happened. We got a call on a domestic. It was a couple fighting; a white male and white female. We arrived to find them both drunk and bleeding, rolling around on their front porch. Do you know that they refused to let us help them. Granted, they couldn't stop us from doing anything since a crime had been committed, but they really didn't want our help. Not because they were afraid of us but because we were black. The white male (husband) said to me, he didn't want the help of an *affirmative action Nigger* and spit on me. He was my first arrest.

I'm tired I'll write you later.

Your son, Eli

5.3.92

Dear Professor:

Training is over! I have been assigned to work in district 8. It's supposed to be the worst area of the city; it's predominantly black. There will be no more Otis and his fishing stories. I've been assigned a permanent partner. Quincy Iverson, he seems to be a good man. He grew up in district 8. Quincy is about 5'1" and 280lbs. He's separated from his wife. 8 hours riding in a car with someone you'd be surprised what becomes the focus of discussion. Well, maybe you wouldn't. I don't know.

It was pretty slow last night. There were people out trying to buy beer and wine before the bewitching hour of 1:00am, when they stop selling. They reminded me of a story you told me once. A Greek myth about the Shades of Hades; you would read to me as if I were one of your students. Like the Shades these people seemed formless, mere reflections of humanity. The alcohol is the thing giving them a human quality. A quick taste and the numbness will be gone; color returns to the cheeks, joy and mirth, shaking the appearance of the damned apparition.

I thought about what I told you last time about how white people treated me. You know, it's worse with black people. I can see the hate in their eyes when we patrol the neighborhood. Some have even thrown rocks and shot at us. I'm okay though.

Eli

5.11.92

Dear Professor:

Momma called me she said she doesn't understand why I write. Why I just don't call? She said she has seen a few letters when checking the mail but she doesn't open them because they are addressed to you only. She said you never discuss the letters with her though she assumes you read them because you pick them up no sooner than she brings the mail in. But she couldn't be certain and that I should know you by now and you hold things deep.

Maybe, sometime soon you and Momma can come into the city and we can have lunch or dinner. I know it's rare for you to come in town anymore but maybe this time.

Love
Eli

5.18.92

Dear Professor:

I have noticed when you meet people for example in a public place, trains, markets, on the street, I can see myself so completely. We all have the same dreams and ambitions: trying to get from point A to B. I guess I am saying we are all the same.

I'm no better than the people I arrest, with or without an education.

Eli

5.25.92

Dear Professor:

I should have known sooner or later that adolescent shadow of police ritual would cast itself over me.

I walk into roll call and the conversational chaos fills the room in no unusual manner. I take my seat mid room and the class clown leans forward from his seat behind me and says loudly, what's happenin' Denzel? He goes on to include the entire room. Stating I look like a movie star but as the milk commercial says I need to drink milk to make my body grow. But the name Denzel stuck. Others began to make comments that I was too small and pretty for this type of work

I'm taller than Quincy by about 7 inches, but he does have me by weight, by about 130 lbs. I understand why they call him Que-ball.

Well anyway the night was strange. We got a 911 to a part of the City they call *The Bottoms*. It was eerie almost surreal the way everything went silent after the siren was turned off and we stepped from the cruiser. I could feel the air against my skin like I had just walked into a cobweb, but the wind was not blowing. The first thing I saw was blood on the sidewalk leading up the porch. This trail led us through the entire house, up to an attic to a child's crib and then to a room of mattresses topped with feces. We looked everywhere and came up empty. We checked all the local hospital ER's for recent injury reports. Nothing. It's crazy.

Eli

6.11.92

Dear Professor:

I had to fight a 200lb naked woman. She had the police at the front door negotiating for the three children she had locked in a room. She said she was going to save them from the Dope Man by stabbing them to death with the assorted kitchen knives she had lined across the coffee table.

I came in through the back of the house through an open window. I followed her voice around a corner and there she stood, Ms. Cellulite. I ordered her down and she turned on me with a butcher knife. I sprayed her with pepper-spray and struck her with my fist and forearm and she crumbled. Quincy and the others kicked in the front door and cuffed her. I went for the kids. The kids said she was their grandmother and she had been up for two days smoking *crack cocaine*.

You know they sent me through the window because the rest of them were too big. I'm okay.

Eli

6.19.92

Dear Father:

The mornings after shift appear to bring with it this a haze of peace or and an sensation of tranquility. It starts right after I turn in my paper work to the shift supervisor, my sergeant. We all stand in the hall while the supervisors review our reports and sign off on them. The conversation is different now. It's nothing like at the beginning of shift. It is subdued, almost reverent to the rising sun breaking over the edge of the cityscape and through the fifth floor window where we congregate. I know we are all somewhat sleep deprived but it's not fatigue that changes my posturing or theirs. I believe it is just the silence that always occurs as a new day births.

Instead of discussing money, sex, getting drunk or heckling someone we tend to sustain one another. Almost like love, but a more peculiar emotion that affords us a particular type feeling of kinship. A feeling of closeness because we have lived through another night. And it is at this point that all those things that separated us at the beginning of shift diminish into that morning mist. That bond seems to build with every morning after.

Once I get home the solace grows, expanding in the silence of my apartment. I catch myself sometimes, tip-toeing around not to disturb the holiness of the hour. I write you in this time in the serenity of the morning silence and then I sleep.

Before I sign off I heard Paula has finished her PhD. That's great! Well at least one of your children is following in your footsteps.

Love you,
Eli

6.20.92

Dearest Father:

I know I haven't mentioned much about Alicia and how she is fairing through this change of career. We rarely ever discuss, communicate, articulate anything about my relationships. I know you have always allowed a vast amount of freedom in that area of my life. Now Paula on the other-hand…no I'm kidding. You've never once invaded that aspect of our lives unless we have come to you.

Well, I'm coming to you now. After two years Alicia decided very abruptly that she couldn't be a part of my life. She said something had changed between us. In someway I'm relieved because it's hard for me to imagine myself married or even planning to be in one. She told me after she finishes graduate school she's going back to Albuquerque to spend time with her family and if I get tired of playing cops and robbers let her know. She graduates with Paula. I do miss her sometimes. I miss the way she'd curse at me in Spanish when I'd frustrate her. New Mexico is a long way from Chicago. What could Alicia think has changed, except the obvious, my choice of occupation. She said I have lost my ability to feel. Feel what? I know your thinking it's the job, but it's not.

Your Son

6.28.92

Dear Dad,

Remember Swanko? He got caught molesting a mentally retarded woman in the paddy wagon. I'm sure you'll see it in the newspaper.

Sometimes I feel like everything is so completely dark. I mean, lately I've been feeling like the enemy, the bad guy, the criminal, every time I put my uniform on.

I wish I could pull the sky down and wrap myself up in the world and disappear for a while. Anyway write me back.

Love,
Eli

6.30.92

Dad,

I pulled this kid from a burning car. He was drunk and crashed into a telephone pole. His family is trying to sue me, stating I dislocated his shoulder when I pulled him from the wreck. It took the Fire Department so long to get there that the car was completely engulfed in flames, popping and sparking but nevertheless...I should have left him.

You said to me, teachers could reshape the world by the impact they have on the students they teach. What about the people that will never make it to the classroom? Who will help reshape their world?

Eli

7.2.92

Dear Dad,

Sometime ago I wrote you commenting on a conversation I had with Momma. She mentioned something about you feeling things deeply or rather holding things deep. I know you do. I know because of all the times you have been there, through broken arms and 100-degree temperatures and first days at new schools. How many first graders get their lunch catered by their father who also stays to eat with them? The bullies didn't think it was so great but I did. I took that ass-kicking proudly. I'm kidding, no one beat me up because you came that day but because they were in awe.

How do you feel now? I know what you would say about me joining the police force but how do you feel?

Your Son,
Eli

7.4.92

Dad,

We pulled into the Safeway gas station, we always stop there at the beginning of shift. The *Baby Blues* (that's us) preferred Pepsi and Hostess Cupcakes, the yellow kind, rather than the coffee and donuts the *Old Blues* seem to require. Quincy exited first. He liked flirting with the cashier. I stayed to give our location to the dispatcher. I watched Quincy laughing and talking to a young kid from the neighborhood, standing at the entrance of the store. I put the handset down and then I heard several pops. I thought, it's the fourth and just some kids lighting firecrackers. And then I saw Quincy running towards the cruiser waving his arms, his gun out. I pulled out mine while at the same time I called out the signal on my shoulder microphone, exiting the vehicle. By the time the door shut behind me Quincy was crawling, not running. The kid was running, tripping over his baggy pants. The kid dropped and rolled to his back aiming a gun at me.

They shot Quincy. The kid shot Quincy...from his own neighborhood...because he doesn't like police.

I killed him, right there on the pavement not far from the gas pumps and where Quincy had fallen. Right there, with people passing by on their way home or even to work. I killed him right there.

Eli

9.8.92

Dad,

They gave me a commendation, an award for taking a life. How much does one life mean? How much should life mean to me? They gave me a new partner too. I guess that's how much a life means, about as much as a replacement cost to train and put in this polyester; about $29,500.00.

Anyway, I wish you could have met Quincy he was a lot like William. He was street-wise but he still maintained a level of innocence. It was in that way that he reminded me of Will. I haven't seen Will since I became a cop. No, that's not true I saw him once and he avoided me like he owed me money.

I was in ACME buying some groceries and I ended up behind him in the check out line. I spoke and he gave a big smile and then it melted. He asked me if true that I was a cop? I showed him my badge and he got out of line and left the store. We've been friends, god since high school. We used to get together at least once a month before I joined the force.

Anyway, my new partner name is Shawn Foster and they call him Tallboy. He's like a tall lanky version of me only more athletic and less cerebral. He's a few years younger than me; just getting out of the Navy. We hang out off duty and Tallboy can drink with the best of them. Watching him drink makes me see how much my own drinking has picked up.

By the way Paula sent me an invitation to her Doctoral Commencement, maybe I'll see you there.

Eli

10.2.92

You know,

The day seems almost non-existent for me. It's almost like a dream filled with mundane doings. It is as if paying my bill's existent only in illusion; going to the Electric Company seems such nominal entertainment compared to what happens at night. How can writing a check be real in comparison to walking into a house where a couple has been fighting. The house is clam when we arrive. The woman explains what has happened to Tallboy. The man wishes to explain to me. We separate the couple. The man turns to walk into the next room and it's then I notice the steak knife sticking out of his back. On another occasion a drunk led us into an alley where he'd been sleeping lately stopped us. He's upset because someone has been messing with his stuff. He shows us a dumpster and we find a 16 year old dead girl wrapped in a blanket, inside. The water bill, holidays, family are illusions.

I couldn't make Paula's graduation I had to work.
Eli

10.15.92

Hey,

I went on a call last night and it was just an average call, nothing out of the ordinary. A simple report. But I was completely inspired by victim. A woman named Bena. I could barely take the report. She had been involved in an altercation with an ex-lover and his new one, nothing serious. She has an odd intensity about her aside from the fact she is fine. She's like the link between my realities, the dream of day and the truth of night. I wasn't sure how I could talk to her outside the job but when Tallboy and I were leaving the scene I noticed the car in the driveway and it's door ajar. There was a purse still on the front seat. I went back to let someone in the house know. Bena answered the door and I asked her if I could call her.

Eli

12.1.92

It's been a while,

    I haven't written much since Bena moved in with me. There's no more day for me, only night. I was wrong about Bena, wrong about her linking my realites. She has completely severed them. One cut off from the other becoming a memory of a former life. If not up all night with work I'm up all night with her. Her intensity goes from extreme adulation to violent paranoia. Sometimes I find myself following the same course, just to communicate. When I drink my emotions run in a manic fashion, but it's become one of my only pleasures, to drink. I'm all right I guess, everything just seems weird, upside down. Always tension. I work a lot and Bena is at home alone most nights and I guess that could cause tension. Maybe all this is too real, I mean this job, this woman I'm with. It could all be a little too real or consequential.

    The other night I was leaving for work and Bena walked me to the door. I inhaled and the night-air and told her it smelled like death in the air. I don't know why I said it. She kissed me and told me she loved and to be careful. The first call of the night was a double homicide, not uncommon. But the thing that struck me was the crime scene. People and cops stood around these two bodies in the street laughing and talking, this too is common place. But here's the thing, here was this dog, wagging it's tail, jumping around playfully and then it bopped over to the bodies, sniffed one and then the other and fell over on it's side, took four short breaths and died. It was almost as if death was truly something to smell and the dog, he could smell it, like he can hear sounds that we can't. I'm sure dogs can smell things we can't. Anyway, nothing was said about the dead dog. I tried to talk to Tallboy about it but he said, so what, why worry you ain't dead.

    Maybe he was right, I was making too much of it. Everyone else carried on unaffected. The two cadavers plus the k-9 were only acknowledged to avoid stepping on them. But of course indifference is the cop way.

    Well, I'm going to try to sleep after I wake Bena for work. Sleeping hasn't been easy lately.

Eli

1.7.93

Tallboy and I made the news last night. I know someone in the family had to see it, high-speed chase down Lakeshore Drive. The driver crashed his car into the shore embankment. Then he jumped and started stripping his close off. He swallowed the dope he had in his possession and had an allergic reaction. It took us a few minutes to reach him and by the time we did he was already butt naked and freezing.

Later that night a drunk spit on me. We stopped him because he was staggering in the street. I lost it and beat him severely. That wasn't me I kept trying to tell myself while transporting him to the hospital. Then, I tried to convince myself with the encouragement of fellow Officers that the drunken man deserved it. Even the doctors and nurses believed this man had these contusions and lacerations coming to him because of his drunk belligerent state. But I knew he didn't though I agreed with everyone else.

Happy New Year!
Write me back for once.
Eli

1.17.93

I can't stand Bena. It just seems like she complains about everything, always angry or scared about something. It was fun and exciting at first, all the craziness with arguing and making-up. The over exaggerated jealousy, I thought I could handle and I wanted too because she's beautiful. But if I want fight I can go to work for that, I don't want to come home to it. She's really no different than the people on the street. I mean, I guess she's just like those people. That's how I met her. Sometimes it's cool to be out here with Bena and with all that life has to push at you but you can get tired.

Bena through a fit because I wanted her read something on one occasion and on another she started throwing dishes because I thought it be good for her to go college. It's like falling to earth or going to a foreign country and suddenly your ability to speak the language is limited. Or when you do speak your accent gets in the way. I'm Robinson Crusoe and Bena is Friday with an attitude. I'm living in complete darkness and Bena my *light* is a black hole. How can you tell someone, stop you're killing me when they can't understand what you're saying.

Tallboy was off last night and I didn't make too many friends by stopping the beating of man that had fifty-dollar loud music warrant. My fellow officer's had gone so far as to kicking the man in the mouth breaking teeth. I couldn't take the sound of police issue boots hitting his face, so I stopped it. I guess the man filed a complaint and sued.

Eli

2.10.93

I told Bena it's not working and she asked me did I really want someone else touching her? I told her I needed to go and she swallowed a bottle of pills. So I stayed, at least until now. Every week she's pregnant or getting an abortion or wanting to die or joining a church it seems. I put my new address on this envelope. I'm supposed to meet Tallboy at this new club but I think I've had enough to drink for today.

Eli

3.8.93

Paula,

I'm sorry I missed the graduation. Mom said things are going well for you. I'm happy for you, Doctor. Good luck at the University and I hope to see you soon.

Eli

3.8.93
Dear Alicia,

Congrats on graduating. I know this letter is a little late. I hope you and your family are well and in good health. You have great mind and a great body, just kidding. It 's true but I'm kidding. I know you'll be successful no matter what you decide to do.

My sister told my mother she saw you at a recent conference or workshop or something. I guess you're seeing someone. That's good. I wish you the best.
Eli

3.25.93

I've taken a couple of days off for personal time. I had to because ever since that incident with the guy getting his teeth knocked out I've been on the black list. Cops don't want to work with me. Some have even threatened me. Tallboy is still with me but they aren't making it easy for him either.

I started reading some of my old school books. Bena used to drop every now and again but I suspect she's found someone to focus her affections on. So it's my books and me. I know I said I ended it between us but letting go is easier said than done.

It seems a life time ago when I could talk to someone about anything beyond, getting paid, getting laid, getting splayed (drunk or high). I miss our talks.

I needed to take this time before I let somebody get killed or before I killed somebody. I was so distracted that I'd be sitting in the cruiser with the radio on full volume and not hear them calling our car number. I started forgetting things. The other night I forgot my gun at home. It's happened to others but that's no excuse. I need to get together. One good thing, nobody noticed because I covered my holster with my jacket. When shift started I called out a 'one', which is a code for general purposes like getting gas for the cruiser or going to the bathroom, instead I went home to get my gun.

Eli

4.16.93

Tallboy was driving last night and a call went out. I didn't hear it because I was asleep. He woke me when we got on scene. It was Bena's mother's house. I didn't realize this until I was standing at the front door. Her mother answered, frantic and angry. I didn't know that they had specifically requested our car until Tallboy mentioned it as we entered the house. He was smiling.

Bena sat in the chair she was standing by the first time I met her. Her level of intensity still burned. She was somewhat battered and wild. She looked at me and said, he raped me, raped me. I said, who? Her mother said, that dirty sumbitch and pointed to a picture of her husband, Bena's stepfather. We found him in a drunken sleep in the screen house off the back patio. He was lying face down on the ground. Bena kept looking at me saying I didn't believe her. I said nothing.

We arrested her stepfather for drunk and disorderly and told them to file the rape charges with the prosecutor's office while the stepfather sobered up.

I don't know if he did it, I don't want to know. I don't want to know how it's going to end. One thing about the night, people don't realize, just like too much light can make you blind, so can darkness. You go blind.

Eli

4.17.93

Today I gave them my gun. For some it would have been like giving up a million-dollar lottery ticket or giving up the keys to the world. I guess in some ways it was. Maybe if those keys had opened up more than just the basement doors I would have been less inclined to part with them.

The minute the equipment supervisor touched my gun I became invisible. No one even saw me leave the building. I don't think anyone even remembers my name, do you?

Eli

Seconds

I heard about it on the radio, in my car, on my way to work. Everything was static, garbled but her name sounded with precise clarity. I reached for the radio and tried to replay it as if I had some control over airwave frequencies. I repeated her name aloud not thinking of the tragedy that surrounded it.

I had not realized I was pulling into the parking deck at the bank. My eyes refused to focus and my hands couldn't feel the steering wheel. I was crying, crying for Rachel. Stray imagines of Rachel tumbled heavily like loose rock on a mountain slope.

I began thinking of our wedding day. There were white roses and calla lilies garnishing the sanctuary of the church and lace streamers hanging delicately along the pews leading to the pulpit.

I stood in place, my eyes seeing only her. She moved with grace and bearing holding a bouquet of two white roses and a single calla lily. Her hair against the white veil looked less like hair but black silk. Her eyes stayed; looking hard into mine, and with each step, it became apparent they would not veer.

The image shatters, and tumbling recollections pummel the fragile introspection, she is asking me to stay home but instead I go out with friends. Another stone smashed through, wrapped in coming in at 7:00am after being out all night, finding dinner in the microwave. And another stone, calling home from a bar and she does not answer. I remember going home and finding a strange car in the driveway. Driving to a pay phone, calling again, and she answered sounding as if she were in a deep sleep. I told her I was wondering why she had not called my pager and it had *me* worried. Normally, when I was out she would page me to see when I was coming home. Though my answer would always be, *I'm on my way*, meaning hours later. This night she said she decided just to go sleep. "Look, I am on my way, this time", I told her. The silence swallowed me in its thickness as I drove back home. I could feel the tension knotting the muscles in my back the closer I got the driveway. The vehicle was gone and I breathed out but I could not breath in so the road did stop for me, I kept driving.

Customers casually walk in to handle their banking business, and I smile, and they smile back with no more trust in that gesture than if they were looking at the back of my head. And the stones keep falling, weighting me down, but not filling me up. The heaviness plummets with an echo into the hollowness, *the emptiness* of my spirit. It is as if I hunger but my belly is full. Full of the weight of our marriage—Rachel and I never divorced, though I have not seen her in 2 years.

A young lady stood at my desk. She is opening a mutual fund. She maybe as old as Rachel had been at the time of our meeting. I worked at another branch then, a teller. She and Rachel had the same face, angular and sharp, smoothed over by copper skin. She, like Rachel had brown eyes that spoke of gentle trust. I wondered what Rachel looked like now. Her *cop* boyfriend had beaten her the night before, after an incident at a strip-club, where she presumably had been dancing. He'd broken her jaw.

I could not believe it. I didn't want to believe it. It pressed against my head, but I wouldn't let it in. I didn't want to. I didn't want to know. I had heard rumors and even had some remote suspicion. And that suspicion I put in a place in my mind where things don't get defined, but felt. I could feel it but I couldn't speak it. I told myself Rachel is a *free spirit*, uninhibited, but she wouldn't go that far.

But it's taken place and here I am opening a mutual-fund account for this young woman, who very well could be rushing off at night to the nearest strip-club to give lap dances for strangers waving dollars. Maybe having dollars stuck between your thong and a little soliciting did more than a mutual fund could.

The last customer moved to the exit and the clock on the wall read 3 o'clock. A sigh comes from the weight pushing on my chest and I drop my head on the desk. I crumbled like weathered sandstone. I stand and collect the assorted forms that lay in front of me. I filed them away in the proper place, neatly as I had done so many things in my life.

I made my way to the parking deck. There is a couple walking by laughing. Their delight seemed to be shared at first. A couple having a moment, it appeared. But then, it became altogether separate; she laughing at something known only to her and he responding in ignorance with his most confident comedy.

Perhaps my attention is heightened, but my perspective flawed because I was thinking about Rachel and in the *woman* I could hear her.

I get to my car without any further events. Starting the engine then begin to drive. I think of going to the hospital where Rachel is listed in satisfactory condition. Instead, I turn into Lou's Bar. I often went to Lou's after work. Why should today be any different?

The door squeaked as I pushed it in. I didn't recognize any of the faces around the bar. The bartender I knew. My shoes stuck to the floor as I approached an empty barstool. The bartender wiped the section of counter in front of me.

"Guinness?"

I nod, adjusting myself on the maroon vinyl. I sip the thick-black, frothy brew tasting its bitterness and finding it pleasant. I could see myself across the bar in the mirror that stretched its length. I stare at my features, thinking I should get a haircut and trim my goatee. Lou's, I like. There is no pool tables, no dance floor but they did have a jukebox, along with a few tables and chairs. Lou's isn't a place of escape for me. It is a place free of distraction. I would come to Lou's every Thursday, drink two beers and go home. I never notice faces. I never look. Today I look and catch a glimpse of something familiar.

It is shape and movement. Someone moving passed me, behind me, a woman moving toward the jukebox fondling a cigarette. Her shape is large and full, though she moves with confident ease. Her haircut is close to her head and her ears stretch slightly by the weight of the bangle earrings. She stares, reviewing carefully the jukebox menu. Her complexion is fair but the glare from the neon-light beaming up from the jukebox makes her pale. She smacks her lips together and without putting a coin in turns away.

"Y'all ain't got nothin'", she said aloud. She eyed the bartender and then me. I knew her. She was from the old neighborhood. I had also seen her in here a few times before but I never said anything to her. Her demeanor is fixed by means of inebriation. We made eye contact and she sways over to me, "You got a light?" Her eyes cast down. She looks up, "Hey I know you, you ol' school from the eastside," she said pausing. She eyes me up and down and nods like she knew something," You know, ah girl I went to school wit, from our neighborhood got messed up pretty bad last night…I heard her nigga' flipped on her. You know she was strippin' and I heard she was ho'in' too an…an…an he busted her up pretty bad."

I don't say anything at first, "You mean Rachel Morgan? Yes, I heard about it."

She sits down at the bar beside me. The maroon vinyl disappeared leaving the impression she was balancing herself on a pole.

"Whatchu' drinkin'?" she said

"Beer." I offer to buy her one and I watch her drink it straight down. "You decided to talk to me today, uh…what, just to tell me about Rachel?"

"Y'all was togetha' wasn't y'all?" she said nodding in agreement with herself. She wipes her mouth with her arm; lifting it high enough to see her armpit needed shaving. She isn't wearing a bra and her breast sag. She is fixing her spaghetti-stringed top; the left strap keeps falling off her shoulder. She leans over pushing her breasts together, increasing her cleavage with her arms, "You an her ain't togetha' now… so, you got any body?"

I moved a little away from her and said, "Yes, I do but thanks, here have another beer…I need to be going."

"I'll walk you to yo' car," she said and picked up the money from the bar I offered for the beer. She palmed it and then tucked in her pocket. We start walking.

"What do you think you gon' do?" she asked me. "You gon'go see her, she right over at Presbyterian Hospital."

She is irritating me.

"I haven't seen Rachel in almost two years, what would be the point now? There's nothing I can do for her."

"Yeah, I mean that's a long time. Wasn't you married or somethin'?"

"Yeah."

"Ain't nothin' you can do, nope not for ol' Rach."

She is grinding against my thigh and my nerves.

"I was trippin' when I heard about it. Rach was one of them smart girls. Like you, smart. She could have got out the *block*. Like you did. Cain't believe she went out; she was too smart to go out like that. Smart and pretty too."

"She must have thought so too," I said harshly, "that's how she ended up in the hospital. What about you...you smart too?"

She stepped back, letting her hand drop from stroking my shoulder.

"Naw I ain't smart I never did get out the *block*...at least Rachel got out witchu'...why she come back I..."

"I really don't want to hear this. We all make our choices. We gotta' live with them." I sounded like a hard-ass, cold, and I felt bad for being that way. I'm sure this woman didn't choose to live as she did. I asked, "What do you think she'll do...when she gets out...out of the hospital?

She remained quiet, staring down at her hands. "It's strange," she said, sounding as if we were old friends, "I used to think Rachel was better-n-me but we just the same. Thas' what I kept thinkin' when I heard."

"What do you mean the same?"

She looked at me with an empathic expression, as if I were 3 years old and had scraped my knee.

"Scared to leave the *block*...no matter how bad it gets, at least there you can count on shit bein' fucked up. You can count on the day beginnin' and endin' just like that. And if you turn out not tah never do shit in yo' life, it don't matter cause ain't nobody on the *block* shit anyway."

"You believe that?"

She let out a breath and put her hands in her pockets. She pulls the money for the beer out and hands it to me.

"Here" she said.

I could feel the stones shifting inside of me, the heaviness returning. I looked away from her extended hand.

"Here's yo' money back...for the beer."

"No, that's okay keep it."

She put it back in her pocket.

"Thanks."

We reach my car.

"Well, I better go."

"Is gon' be hard on Rach," she said.

"Yeah, well you take care." I got into my car. She stood there until I pulled off.

I didn't go see Rachel. And it is sometime before I mailed the get-well card. It is right after I am promoted to Executive Director of Financial Planning. She sent me a card for my birthday. It said, "happy birthday, love Rachel. P.S. I'll be released from the hospital soon. When I am I'll need a ride."

I held the birthday card letting the words blur in front of my eyes. I couldn't see the words but I could see Rachel walking towards me in her black strapless evening gown. It was New Years Eve and I had purchased tickets to the city celebration. She was beautiful and happy. We had been married a year. I watched her check her make-up and I smiled knowing that we had just made love moments earlier. I was thankful that I decided a year earlier to take route 8 instead of the main road to work. The traffic was jammed because of an accident. It was hot and people were standing outside their vehicles complaining. When traffic came to a stop we happened to be right beside one another. I was sweating and she was laughing at me from her air-conditioned car. She rolled her window down and asked me if it was hot enough. I smiled and opened the can of Mountain Dew I'd been saving for lunch.

Her eyes bulged and she motioned that she was thirsty. I asked her was it hot enough for her. And now she's here, my wife, she'd always be my wife. As the New Year came we promised never to divorce. I guess that's one promise we kept even after all this time.

I left a message with the front desk of the hospital and they informed Rachel I would be there. I arrived a few minutes early. I watched her come off the elevator. She is thinner than I remember. She hasn't lost her ability to move gracefully. She sees me standing in the lounge adjacent to the exit. A grin brakes across her face showing the wires that hold her jaw in place. Her eyes look tired, but remain youthful. I, more or less forgot I didn't know her. I didn't know this Rachel.

"Ssho 'ow you been?" she asked through metal and spit.

"Good…you okay to talk?'

"Shyeah," she blinked, smiling, her eyes twinkling. "Issh nice-ssh to shee you."

"Yes, you too." The conversation is contrived and uncomfortable.

Rachel looked ageless. It is obvious she is no longer in her early twenties but it is clear her life has not yet taken its toll on her looks, wired jaw and all.

I take her bag and help her into the car. I begin driving, keeping my eyes on the road. I want to look at her and pour out the weight of questions that burden me.

"You still like to swim?"

She smiles, "Umhm. But not since Chapel Hill."

"Neither have I. No time really" I said.

When we first married, we moved into a condo in Chapel Hill. Chapel Hill is the kind of place where the houses where always beautiful and the yards manicured but you never see the people who live in them. And everyday after work we would swim. She behaved as if the pool is some cleansing source. If an argument starts she grabs a towel and heads for the pool. When she returns she is renewed, anointed by something, a peace or greater sense of it.

I think she found it insufferable that I couldn't believe in her act of baptism.

"Where am I taking you?" I asked.

"My Ma's" she said. "Make a left up here."

"I remember how to get there." I said.

"I wasn't sure...you forgot to come home for two years...shit," she said with the back of her head facing me.

The old neighborhood flooded into the car. Familiar shapes and shadows moved inside me. The street narrated what I'd missed. Manor House, a two story apartment building with beaten down grass giving the appearance of a balding man. People siting on the front steps, some silent watching, others holding brown paper bags while still others throwing dice at the ground, screaming obscenities. The street cracks under the car's tires. It's the broken glass. The glass scattered over the pavement in front of Mister Pantry's Carry out. No matter who you are you could be guaranteed two things going in there. One that the Arabs would sell you beer no matter your age, and two, that you'd come out smelling like fried chicken.

Nothing had changed. Young boys and girls still stood fearlessly on street corners, some with jewelry flashing and athletic foot wear looking as if it had just come out the shoebox. I looked at Rachel but she kept her eyes straight ahead.

"Make a right here,"she said.

"I remember," I said.

For a brief moment it felt like no time had passed at all. We were right back in it. The turn came easy. I didn't have to drive slow to read the house numbers, I knew where to go. I knew before I turned. I knew she wasn't going in once I pulled into the driveway.

"Max still driving those big rigs uh?" I saw the truck her stepfather drove parked in the grass.

"Yeah", she said sounding distant.

The door opened and Max came out carrying a gym bag. He walked toward his truck. He saw us and waved politely. The door opened again and Rachel's mother stumbled out. She was mouthing something when she noticed us. Max escaped into the cabin of the truck. She walked over to us and tapped on the window. Rachel rolled the window down, "Hey Ma."

"They let you out today? Oh thas' nice." Her mother began, "Where you been hidin' Mister man? You got a crow bar?"

"Ah, yes in the trunk...you need it?" I said.

"Yep, um gettin' ready to bash this niggas head in."

Rachel's mother said pointing at Max in his truck.

"Let's go." Rachel said.

"Go where?" I said.

"Just go!" she said.

We drove to my house in silence. I pulled into the garage letting the car idle.

"Your Ma' still trippin', huh?"

She ignored me.

"When'd you move here?" she said.

"I've been here a while...Tell me why'd you leave the bank?"

"You don't know? You tell me how I'm suppose to work when everybody knows that your husband can find his way to work everyday but he can't find his way home!"

"Why would I come? There was no room for me." I said.

"What? No room, room for what?"

I turned the car off and got out.

"Why did you ask me to come get you? I mean after all this time?"

"Because you sent me the get-well card."

"Why did you come?"

"I guess I wanted to know if you had changed? I mean circumstances change but people don't always..."

"I need a place to stay tonight...I'll go to my Ma's tomorrow. The drama should be over. Max will be on the road."

***

A slamming door woke me. I rolled off the couch, tossing my blanket to the side. I stood straightening my sweat pants. I looked in the kitchen and nothing had been disturbed. I walked into the bedroom and opened the door slowly, knocking softly. The bed had been turned but no Rachel. I checked the bathroom and finally the study and still no Rachel. I heard the patio door slide. I moved with silly excitement back to the kitchen. Rachel stood barefoot on the tiled floor, dripping in my black swim trunks and T-shirt. She was rubbing her hair with a towel.

"That was great. Now I'm hungry," she said.

"I see you found the pool."

I couldn't conceal the fact I was pleased.

"Yeah, now I need to find some food."

"I think there's some soup up there you can eat…when I get dressed we can go to the store."

"For real…this soup is the only thing you got up here. Do you eat?"

"Yeah I eat."

"But not everyday uh?" she laughed.

"We'll go to the store and get some stuff." I said.

"I need a swimsuit too, Evan."

I listened to her say my name like she'd given it to me at birth. I almost envied her. I envied what water could do. I looked at her and smiled because I knew that she had washed herself free. For me there was only one way to straighten out something crooked, something bent and water couldn't do it. If the road were crooked I'd just have to dig it up and relay it. But for her water flowed over and through, penetrating everything and as she came up from the deluging depths, breaking the surface of the liquid cure, her sin now left at the gesturing underside making her free.

***

Being in the grocery store brought back an avalanche of memories. The stones inside me shifted and piled with each isle we turned down. It was like traveling roads to the past, each a different place in history reflecting and connecting emotion to imagery.

We turned from frozen food to bath and body. I remembered the embarrassment I felt carrying the Tampax pads through the checkout counter because Rachel for some reason or another could not pick them up herself.

"Rach!" A voice broke through my memories.

"Rachel!"

"Lamont?" Rachel answered.

A stocky balding man approached us.

"Hey babe, ah been callin' yo mom's…you ain't call when you got out? I figured you was still mad about what all happened…"

"Lamont what are you doing here? Rachel asked.

"Ah had to pick-up some stuff for ma moms…you know she stay close to this store…who dis? Yo step brother you always tellin'me about?"

"I heard you were locked up." She said.

"Bratha had to make bail", Lamont smiled under the influence of some strange pride. "I really ain't supposed to be talkin' to you…"

"I know there's a restraining order out until the court date is over."

"Ah babe you know I'm sorry, I'm sorry for what happened…who'd you say this is?"

"This is Evan. Evan this is Lamont."

I watched the expression on Lamont's face twist then drain into his fist.

"Evan as in yo' ex-husband Evan?" Lamont's eyes bulged.

"Yes." She said in a way that well could have been a gun going off in Lamont's face.

"What the fuck you doin' wit' dis nigga'?"

Though I didn't like being called a nigga' in the way he meant it I had to ask myself the same question. …Why is she with me?

"Lamont I suggest you go on before you get into more trouble." Rachel said.

"Fuck you Rachel, you's a ho," Lamont pushed by me taking Rachel's advice.

"That's your boyfriend?" I said smiling and feeling superior. "He's alittle on the fat and balding side, huh?"

"That's my husband and screw you Evan!" She turned pushing the cart to the next isle.

"Wait, hold on a minute…husband? I thought I..we were…" I ran up behind her.

"I divorced you a year ago on the grounds of abandonment." She said with the same tone she used with Lamont. I heard the *bullet* go passed my head. I was silent through the check out line and to the car and the drive home. It wasn't until I was standing in the kitchen that I realized how much time had elapsed without a single word to Rachel.

Rachel was standing beside me dumping ice cream in the blender. "Hand me that bottle of lemon abstract…please." She reached in front me brushing me slightly. I moved the bottle. "Stop playin' and give it here," she sounded playful and adolescent. "The ice-cream is going to melt...Evan."

I handed the small bottle to her, but when she grabbed it I didn't let go.

"You want to play now...huh? I guess you over your little temper tantrum? You left me remember?"

I let the bottle go. "It only takes a second to change a life...to forget something of the past. Seconds for something to happen and be forgotten." I said.

I walked out on the patio. I watched the water shimmering under the shrinking sun.

"Hey, you want some of this milk shake?" Rachel's voice called from behind.

"No thanks." I watched her walk and sit down beside me.

"It's nice out, huh?" She said. "So where's the new Mrs. Evan at anyway?"

"There's no one." I said.

"Evan please, I know you well enough to know there is someone. Who is she?"

" I go out but it's nothing serious. She teaches over at the University."

"You always liked them smart. Is she pretty? No, don't tell me just show me because I know you've got picture of her somewhere."

"How do you know that?"

"Because you collect things. Women are things to you." Rachel stood up.

"I'll go grab the photo. I don't collect things. I mean I do collect books but you know that...and some art...But women?" I said attempting to defend my nature. I came back and Rachel was standing at the edge of the pool. I handed the picture to her and took my seat.

"Pretty. I guess you gave up on sista's? Because she definitely *ain't* black." Rachel turned looking back at me. "What is she? She's not White either. Is she mixed or something?"

"Or something...she's Hispanic."

Rachel flipped the picture at me and jumped into the pool. I watched her disappear and reappear in short splashes of hands and kicking feet. She swam to the opposite edge of the pool moving with an aquatic precision, beautiful. She paused as she came up pushing her hair back away from her eyes, wiping the water off her face with her palm in a downward motion. She looked across the water at me and climbed out.

"Thanks for the swimsuit." Rachel walked toward me picking up her towel her feet slapping against the cement. She leaned slowly, "I do love you," and she kissed me on the forehead.

I leaned back in my chair trying to hold back the pressing thought, "Rachel who's car was that?"

"What?"

"You know…back then." I said, "The night I didn't come home."

"Which night was that?" Rachel smirked.

"C'mon Rachel."

"Evan I don't know…does it matter?"

"Yes, that night changed everything for both of us."

No, it changed for me. You're still the same, expecting the world to wait on you…to wait for you to grow the fuck up. But it's not like that Evan, too many seconds go by waiting for you."

"Oh, so because of me you started *shaking it* for money?"

"Oh, please Evan my dancing had nothing to do with you…my world does not revolve around you. Don't worry about why I started dancing!"

"What about your husband?" I said.

"What about him?" she said sharply.

"You, here with me," I said.

"It's quiet here…besides it's not like we're having sex."

I cut my eye at her.

"Don't get me wrong I'm still attracted to you. Why? I don't know. But my heart couldn't take it." Rachel spoke softly, running her finger around the edge of her glass then sucking up the remaining milk shake through the white and red striped straw. "It's different with Lamont… he may have broken my jaw but he can never do what you did to my heart…I won't let anyone do that again."

"Oh hell, because I didn't come home? I asked.

"No…because you don't give a fuck!"

"What, aren't you here, now? What about the swimsuit?" She was starting to piss me off, saying I don't care.

"You're right," she said, "I am here and you are kind but it's like a teacher or a doctor or something...they're nice to you, but you never really get to know them."

The phone began to ring keeping me from having to respond to Rachel's accusation that she couldn't get close to me.

"Excuse me for a second, phones ringing." I went inside and she followed.

"Hello, yes speaking. How'd you get this number? I don't care if you are a cop! Look man, don't let being stupid getchu' locked up again. If you love her so much why the hell you beatin' on her? Oh, you gon' beat on me now? Man, there ain't that much love in the world." I hung up and turned towards Rachel, "You need to go home or to your mother's house. I don't need this kind of drama!"

I believed Lamont when he told me he loved Rachel, as crazy as it seems. I knew he felt for her in a way I couldn't. And she is his wife. I'm just a second in history; my moment gone and over.

"Rachel, I don't want that crazy nigga' poppin' up at my front door. You already got this fool illegally gettin' phone numbers and stuff."

"Evan you're in the phone book." Rachel said touching her mouth, "Lamont's harmless Evan."

"He broke your jaw, right?" I said.

"That was an accident; a reflex. I was hitting him."

"I don't give a damn who hit who he's supposed to be able to handle those types of scenes...you *ain't* no bear." I walked toward the patio and though it was dark I could see the top of the wall that separated the patio from the next yard. It was glowing a fluorescent blue, pale and washed out in the light from the pool. The phone rang again. I ignored it and walked out to the pool. I could hear Rachel boasting that no man tells her what to do and if she needed money and dancing was the quickest way for her to get it then she deemed it necessary. And she didn't care what Lamont thought or anyone else for that matter. I yelled back in the house, "Hey, you don't have to justify your actions to me!" jokingly.

"Ain't nobody thinkin' boutchu' Evan...Hell, as broke as we are I can't believe Lamont wanted to trip." Rachel answered from the kitchen.

"I wouldn't like my wife doin' it either!" I yelled back in the house.

" If I were your wife I wouldn't have to." Rachel said now standing in the patio door. We both fell silent and she turned back into the house.

I sat for awhile, still staring at the water. I stood in a robotic fashion. I moved as if pulled by forces outside of me. It was late evening and I had begun to undress. Soon I could feel only the surrounding air against my naked form. I took two steps and my feet left the ground. The world rushed passed my ears, whirling sounds to crashing gurgles, as my body submerged in the coldness of the water.

I drifted face down while bubbles escaped from my nose and mouth. My thoughts seem to wave at me from the bottom, drawing me closer. I touched the bottom surface and it was like landing on another planet. I looked up from my New World seeing a different skyline of quivering images. I reached out and pushed upwards and within seconds I had returned to earth. I waded to the edge preparing to pull myself out of the pool. I blinked my eyes into focus, my arms resting on the cement edge. Rachel stood above me peering down into my face. She was not wearing the new swimsuit. She wasn't wearing anything at all. Her exposed flesh reflected the movement of the water but she did not move and I held on to the edge gazing up.

Rachel smiled gently. I loved her.

"Rachel, I do..." Her eyes moved slowly away from my face aiming at the wall. She jerked and her chest opened up and she tumbled back, falling to the wet cement. I glanced at the wall. Lamont stood at its base holding a gun in his hands and his arms stretched out. I pulled myself out of the pool and tried to stop the bleeding with my hands. Lamont fired again. I turned back to the pool, diving in frantically. The water turned the blood into a crimson smoke. I'd reached the bottom. I was in this other world. I peered up at the surface skyline shifting and rocking. The scribbled imagery played Lamont firing the gun repeatedly into Rachel's body. I knew what this constellation meant in this watery sky. The meaning was easy, man having been following the sky home for ages. I just didn't know what to name it but in seconds I was going to have to explain it.

QUIET DISCONTENT

Cody stumbled, ran and jumped through jobs and careers for what seemed forever. There is no doubt he knew what he wanted at least that is what he would say. But his station in life prevented that level of focus. His most recent and consistent station was broke and unemployed sitting around his apartment hiding from his Landlord. When not faced with his creditors he was thinking of suicide so he would not have to listen to his wife, ex-wife, and now live-in house cleaner. It is not that she was a brutal or hideously ugly on the contrary she was very attractive, though she had picked up a few pounds and was the woman who had loved him since their days in high school.

Cody Styles grew up in a dead industrial city a population of 220,000. The odd thing about that number is it never seemed to change, never going up or down. People could die, move away, go to prison and the number remained at a constant 220,000. Cody did not think much about leaving he just wished the summers would last a little longer. It is said easily that most seven-year-olds felt and thought the same when it came to their warm weather adventures. He loved his yard. It was a place where he could get lost for hours. Hiding under the shade of the great weeping willow, playing super-hero in the grape arbor, chasing the cat up the cherry tree and eating apples that had just fallen from a branch he'd hit, though it may have taken ten tries but finally jumping high enough and swinging at the right moment, he got it.

One day returning from one of his grand adventures he came into the house and mother said, "Cody, this is your cousin Richard." This kid Ricky was different Cody could tell. He wasn't like his other cousin Vincent who lived down the street, who cried and whined taking his ball in the middle of a game whenever things didn't go his way. Ricky was his cousin from California and he seemed to enjoy the adventures of the yard but his attention required more. More than Cody could explain. It was not the type of *trouble making* attention; rather it was his knowledge of life that called for more interest. One day in a seeking fashion Ricky said, "Cody you ever get bored?"

"No." Cody said.

"Do you ever go anywhere?" Ricky asked tossing a plastic star and striped ball to him.

"Go anywhere?" Cody replied throwing the ball back.

"Yeah, go other places." Ricky said.

"For what?"

"To see different stuff."

"Nah." Cody shrugged but his mind began to work.

Summer ended and fall came, then winter and spring, natures chain reaction to man's boredom. This repeated many times and each summer following Ricky's visit Cody's yard grew smaller. Cody was smart, some say too smart for his own good. He started college his junior year of high school, attending high school classes in the morning and college in the afternoon. He played tennis, wrestled, and ran cross-country lettering in all and he had the girl. The *virgin* Denise, maybe the only one left in high school. Denise melted every time Cody breathed. She attended every game and event that Cody was an affiliate, always watching and waiting. Cody among everything else played in a band, writing, leading the songs and exhibiting his paintings in local galleries and Denise was there, with an invariable stare at Cody's every movement. If he looked worried or stressed she would rush to his side seeking to ease his pain. Cody dated many girls even while he dated

Denise, but she always stayed. She became utterly convenient and when they began having sex Cody would never have to ask. He could go out drinking with his friend's and show up at her home at 3:00am and she would feed and make love to him and never ask where he had been. His family loved her. She was perfect for him, *they pushed*, though they perceived her as relatively dull, unassertive and most of all not demanding; her life was his. He just was not sure he wanted it.

Cody graduated college and married Denise. He proposed to her at his graduation party. Traditionally when a member of his family would graduate from college a celebration follows in the Graduates honor. It was during his *thank you* speech to all those who supported him during his college days that he could not take his eyes off Denise. She was beautiful, her ebon hair pulled up letting a single strand fall near her face which disclosed the elegance of her neck shoulders, composed in a white strapless evening gown, showing a hint of cleavage but never distasteful. How could she be less than proper or even pious, she was the daughter of a preacher. Her only flaw was giving into to the sexual ambitions of Cody, who saw himself, now as a thief or bandit who had stolen this *innocence* affections and marred her purity. There she was, again. No doubt, she helped organize the party. He thought about what his father had told him, "Son, you need a woman that will always be in your corner…no matter what…be there for you…Denise is that kind of woman…" He thought about what his mother had said, "Cody, you know Denise loves you…she'll always love you…I don't think you have to worry about her turning on you…she's from good people" According to his parents, a couple married for 25 years, after college marriage was the next evolutionary step for a young person, but for Cody it was protocol.

There were no objections aside from a few disappointed women. This marriage was inevitable. Cody appeared to be robotic through out the entire ceremony, smiling at his brother who had given him a shot of scotch prior to the main event. He told his friends he loved her at least at first.

After the ceremony, they moved into the tiny community where his parents, Aunts and Uncles and Grandparents lived within a minute walk of each other. Cody got an appointment as a congressional aide laying aside his artistic pursuits to don the armor of normal life. Thus it began, the routine of leaving home and returning where she would be with dinner waiting and the following morning she would get up an hour before him and iron his clothes hanging them neatly in the bathroom wardrobe. After some time he started getting all his things dry cleaned, just to keep her from this chore and then she began pressing his underwear and so he stopped wearing those altogether.

Cody would get home and Denise would be busy undressing him and re-dressing him in his lounge coat and slippers. She would run his bath water checking the temperature methodically. Cody recalls one particular winter morning when being awakened by the wind beating the windows and whipping the trees against the house. Denise was already up as usual. Cody saw his tie and shirt hanging pressed to perfection. He dressed and went down for breakfast. Breakfast was on the table with cloth napkins neatly bundled in napkin rings and a set of matching juice and milk glasses filled to the brim. Denise poured every cup, glass, and container to the edge of its lip. This always-bothered Cody, he had asked her to stop pouring his juice but she ignored him. Cody did not read the paper at breakfast but often read abstracts from Nietzsche. Beside his toast lightly buttered with strawberry preserves a book-marked copy of *"Thus Spake Zarathustra"*. Denise was still missing; she always ate with him, discussing his job, money, children, the family, and most things he found of little or no concern. He finished his breakfast and still no Denise. He walked to the washroom noticing the dryer bumping busily finding only traces of where Denise had been. He pulled on the door leading to the garage and a burst of bitter cold wrapped itself around his face causing him to squint. When his eyes stopped watering he could see the garage door was open and Denise shoveling the driveway. She looked up shaking the snow from her hair, "I got the front walk too for the postman," she smiled as she spoke.

"Don't we have someone to do that?" Cody tried not to sound irritated but he was thinking damn the Postman. She looked in his face and saw his displeasure, "Well, I didn't think they'd get here before it was time for you to go to work." She turned back to her labor momentarily disappointed in his reaction. As much as Cody disliked his job, it became a refuge from his wife's love.

A year had passed and nature was still entertaining man's simple survey of 'why' and for Cody 'why' had become a query he ignored. He was afraid to ask or even to feel because if he did he would feel like ripping the petals off the sweetest rose, his wife: the dedicated, devoted, sacrificing, Denise tolerant of all his indiscretions and they were becoming more frequent as she would remind him, letting him know she was his first and only lover yet he trifled with fast women or better said *whores*. Cody attempted church and of course it was with the family and if he were absent, his mother would call and remind Denise for the following week. Cody watched everyone around him, his cousin Vince had settled right into the *evolution of man* according *to the family*. He was a deacon in the church now and still trying to finish his undergraduate degree but the family applauded his tenacious nature and Christian ethic. To Cody Vince was still his punk cousin from down the street that cried when things did not go his way. Cody looked at Vince, his siblings all married with families in this syrupy bliss. This cannot be it, Cody thought.

Denise had become a fixture within his family. It was as if his mother had given birth to her. She was like a sister to Cody not a spouse but an older overly doting sister, they began to debate about everything, and if she needed support for her position, she would call his mother. On more than one occasion, he would go to his parents for resolve and find Denise had already there smiling as if she had won something. Moreover, she had. She had won his parents, his family. It was no longer necessary for her to try to keep up with her father's speaking engagements at area churches, her family was right around the corner and for Cody this meant she was everywhere, closing in on him. He could not breathe and when Friday would arrive, he would find a bar and suck up as much air and alcohol physically possible. He began to dread going home. He begged her to divorce him and she would just hug him and tell him things would work out.

Cody started writing music to stay sane. He leased a small studio space where he would go and create until he was empty. In addition, it was there that he realized nothing he had been doing really mattered. He quit his job and divorced Denise. The family was in an uproar and Denise never acknowledged the fact they were divorced. She did not contest it. She did not show up for court. A jobless musician and divorcee, dear God, poor Denise, these words echoed throughout his family.

Cody was overjoyed until family and friends began to shun him. He was in the most literal sense excommunicated from his family. For some reason he had stopped at his cousin Vince's home and his wife refused to let him in. He called his grandmother she would not speak with him. Someone even told him he was going to hell. Cody's parents alienated him and remarks at family gatherings became so brutal he thought public stoning would soon be an option. Denise became the center of their concerns. It was her family now and she would never be alone. Cody struggled against the pressure of reconciliation. His mother told him as did Denise that nothing would go right for him since he separated from *them*, her. Cody merely responded by saying, "kiss my ass and keep that voodoo hoodoo out of my face."

Things moved along with ease as Cody set out to reconstruct his life. Almost all interactions with his family ceased and if he were dating, his family would never meet the particular young woman because he knew she would have to meet Denise. Denise continued to go to family gatherings and visiting his parents regularly. She merely replaced Cody's roll has her husband with *member* of the family at least until he came to his *right mind*. They all prayed he would one day.

Cody's concerns focused on eating daily, so he took a day job and pursued other interest at night. He could not seem to get away from government work but that was okay because the Civil Rights Commission's liberal attitude suited him. Cody played in a band after hours, mainly on weekends and like clockwork Denise would call once a day and leave a message on his answering machine, offering dinner if he did not feel like cooking or laundry service since he was so busy.

After a gig Cody staggered into his apartment, feeling like his options had just become incredibly unlimited and his phone rang.

"Yes."

"How'd it go?"

"Denise?"

"Yes, who'd you think it was?"

"Honestly I didn't think."

"Do you normally get calls at this hour?"

"What is it woman?"

"I just wanted to know how it went and to tell you goodnight and I love you."

"Okay, whatever."

"Whatever?"

"Denise what is wrong with you? What do you want?"

"I love and miss you?"

"How can you miss me…I never was right by you?"

"You never cared for me?"

"It's not about that…I never cared for me."

"Do you think we…?" she began.

"Why do we have to do this?" he ended.

"Look, I just need someone to have sex with and since I know you…you know I'm not just going to sleep with anyone…nobody else has ever and I don't plan on…"

"It's late, call me later…bye."

Cody hung up trying to figure, should he feel guilty because he did not love her or should he keep *stickin' his business in that chicken?* He needed a clear-cut plan to drive Denise away. He tried infidelity when they were married and it did not work, so that definitely would not work now that they were divorced. He thought maybe if he got deeply involved with someone even let them move into his apartment that would drive Denise away. She would want to stay away then. This worked until it was time for the *newcomer* to meet his family. Denise had them all. The fear of the newcomer meeting Denise was no longer an issue it was the comparing of the newcomer by his parents and the others to the hovering shadow of Denise. Anyone would feel out of place, not welcomed and soon they, would part and Denise would be right there again. It was a conspiracy and Cody was beginning to tire. He felt like a marked man. It was as if he had become a rumor that people often talked about but never gave substance or action to. On the other hand, his family was the Mafia and anyone who dated him would find their lives threatened. Cody loved his family it was all he knew and this made things difficult to separate. No one he knew would come hear him play, before the entire family would come out and support him, not even Denise. Now he was leper. "This is utterly silly, crazy", he would think, "all because I don't want Denise?" One morning he got up preparing for work and realized he had no clean clothes, nothing pressed and nothing to eat. He had been too tired to do laundry and too busy to go grocery shopping. Then he broke. It probably was not the laundry or lack of food but rather the loss of home.

On a Saturday afternoon at *their* mother's church, they married for the second time. Three days later Cody was drunk looking for a bridge and Denise was somewhere smiling humming hymns. Cody sobered up and realized that he had been a coward not to live his life on his own without the security of Denise and her steadiness, her always being there when he did not want to do it for himself. He divorced her but he did not leave her. He quit his job to start his own business and she stayed. He moved away from the family taking Denise, keeping her interaction at a minimum. Denise remained content. Cody packed a duffel bag with a few books and a few clothes that Denise would not miss and put them in the trunk of the car. He thought about Ricky his cousin from California and wondered what he was doing now and how life had faired him and his seeking. Later when Cody got in bed Denise asked him, "Why are you so happy?" He kissed her on the forehead and thought about the bag, closing his eyes in peaceful slumber.